CW01335872

QUILTER'S END

A story of murder, mystery, and reflection

❖

Garry Giles

Copyright © Garry Giles 2025
This book is sold subject to the condition that it shall not, by way of trade or otherwise, be lent, resold, hired out, or otherwise circulated without the publisher's prior consent in any form of binding or cover other than that in which it is published and without a similar condition including this condition being imposed on the subsequent publisher.
The moral right of Garry Giles has been asserted.
ISBN: 9798280033429

To Katie, Dan, and Sarah-Anne for their belief in me.

CONTENTS

CHAPTER ONE 1
CHAPTER TWO 7
CHAPTER THREE 11
CHAPTER FOUR 14
CHAPTER FIVE 21
CHAPTER SIX 24
CHAPTER SEVEN 30
CHAPTER EIGHT 36
CHAPTER NINE 42
CHAPTER TEN 50
CHAPTER ELEVEN 58
CHAPTER TWELVE 69
CHAPTER THIRTEEN 78
CHAPTER FOURTEEN 87
CHAPTER FIFTEEN 96
CHAPTER SIXTEEN 103
CHAPTER SEVENTEEN 112
CHAPTER EIGHTEEN 121
CHAPTER NINETEEN 130
CHAPTER TWENTY 139
ABOUT THE AUTHOR 147

This is a work of fiction. Names, characters, businesses, organisations, places, events and incidents either are the product of the author's imagination or are used fictitiously. Any resemblance to actual persons, living or dead, events, or locales is entirely coincidental.

CHAPTER ONE

❈

Jen had no idea what was about to unfold in her life, and neither did her friends. Leaving what had been a mixture of normalised misery and then a time of apparent safety, she was trying to build a future. That future seemed to be a long time coming but hope was always on her mind. She didn't anticipate the rollercoaster ride of emotions that she would encounter; for the moment, it was about her day job.

Jen was having another busy day in her 'lettings' role. Snow and Co., the estate agent where she worked, hadn't ever seen so many clients. The whole rental market was constantly changing, especially in places like Fenningwood where something like an interest-rate change could produce either an influx of customers, or conversely a lull. With countryside all around and a regular train service into the City of Farcastle, this was commuter land now. Once a village, it was now home to many younger families, and on the east side there was some social housing. She was hoping to get to the library to send an email to her former foster aunt, Kath, though that would have to wait until tomorrow now. She also needed to make a note to get her mobile phone checked as the battery kept running down quickly, though luckily she had the spare phone sent by Aunt Kath in case she needed it. Jen wondered what information may be on Kath's phone but didn't expect to ever bother to find out. At the moment, all she could think about was finishing work and popping to 'The Bunch of Carrots' with a couple of friends for a glass of wine.

Fifty miles away, the police were dealing with a sudden death. They were called to a rather large house named 'Quilter's End' in the village of Lost Whistle, which is about ten minutes or so from the large town of Chrichton. The name of the deceased was Kath Megson, and the police only knew this because the postman identified her and was still there, having phoned them immediately. As was usually the case, Kath's door was open and he handed her mail to her. She eagerly opened a hand-written envelope addressed to her late husband, but as she pulled out the letter inside, it was somehow sealed in an outer coating. Kath went to get some scissors to cut open the letter, wondering why someone would seal post that was already inside an envelope. Then upon opening the letter, which had a small amount of powder inside, with scissors in hand, she keeled over and died. How could her life end so abruptly? The postman took a few steps back.

*

In the 'Carrots', as they called it, Jen saw her friends Dave and Steve and waved a polite greeting to them. They were talking, though she thought nothing of it, trying to put her 'flings' with Steve to the back of her mind, albeit they only amounted to kissing after too many drinks accompanied by some cuddling. She didn't know what it was about Steve, he just seemed to have a smile and aura about him that could so easily break down her barriers. Those barriers weren't ever let down too far, though. She was a bit of a lonely soul in some ways, having not really settled after her foster care finished when she was eighteen years old.

Jen had returned to Fenningwood, though her mum had by all accounts deteriorated in the six years that she had been away. Luckily, she had enough money from a 'start up' grant to find a flat to live in, and also gained a job very quickly. She had been with Snow and Co. for fourteen years now and was earning a decent living with a group of clients that she enjoyed working with. As much as she liked Steve, she couldn't imagine letting someone into her life, as she had become so independent and guarded.

Ironically, Steve was telling Dave how much he fancied Jen, though didn't mention their previous brief encounters. Unknown to Steve or Jen, Dave knew quite a bit about her. But how? He didn't mention anything. Steve confided to Dave that his cleaning business wasn't doing so well. "It's one of those areas that offices cut down on when money is tight. Places that I was cleaning every day are now two, or at best, three days a week. I need to find some money, Dave: that's the truth of it."

Dave nodded, thankful that as a train driver he had a salaried income, although he had to work some grotty shifts to earn that. He said to Steve that he'd noticed him and Jen going out a few times, and that it must be fun.

"It is, Dave, and we've had some great times together. She's lovely company: walking by the river, watching the herons dive in after they've been so still and observant. There's a hard side to her as well, that I don't think other people see. You would need to be alone with her to notice it. When I say 'a hard side', I don't mean that she's nasty or anything, she just has what I think I would call 'a protective shell.'"

Dave was sitting quietly: listening, nodding, and making sympathetic noises. Steve was clearly confused by her.

"I mean, why does Jen go back and forth to the library and never have a book? I don't understand that. While you think about that, I'll go to the bar for refills."

Dave knew exactly why, though would be sharing none of that knowledge. He had often seen Jen in the library, in the reference area. He went to use the computers as he didn't have one at home, which seemed a bit daft to Steve but it was simply because he hadn't got round to buying one and the library made it very easy for him. Jen appeared to be doing the same, though he couldn't work out why. He knew from what she had said in general conversation that she had a laptop at home. So why would she use a library one? He wasn't exactly sure, but his curiosity had started getting the better of him a couple of months ago. He knew that her email address would be easy to find in the history and memory of the computer, but how to find the password? He had found a position where he could watch her hands without her noticing, and slowly, on the occasions that Dave was there at the same time as Jen, he believed he had worked out her password. It helped that she would mouth it as she typed, which gave him an extra check. When the time came to try it, the seat she had been sitting on was still warm. He checked around to make sure that she hadn't forgotten something and might suddenly return.

He immediately felt very self-conscious, as if the others in the library knew that he was about to try and hack into Jen's account. It was like all of them were peeping over their shoulders waiting to see his reaction. Dave wasn't an expressive person so it was unlikely that he would start now. He was ready for his task. On the computer, he went to the last-used address. All he knew of her was that her given name was Jen, presumably short for Jennifer, though nothing remotely recognising this appeared in this email address. Dave decided to give it a try anyway. He sat upright in the armless black office chair and prepared to enter what he believed was the password. *PASSWORD REJECTED* was the reply. Dave looked at the screen in disbelief and let out a long sigh. What had he done wrong?

He looked at what he had written down, then started to rehearse it in his mind. Ideally he would have had a keyboard to use, and he was tempted to try it for tactile reasons but was reticent to move from his seat in case someone else used it and he hadn't jotted down the email address yet. It was when he saw her email address written down that the penny dropped. He had ended her password…q8! And when looking at Jen's email address it should have been…28! He wondered what the significance of 28 was. He retyped the password: he was in! Looking at the short list of emails, he had a moment of guilt. Why was he delving into the affairs of someone that he didn't really know? Yes, he had talked to her many times; he knew where she lived, where she worked, and that she liked Italian rosé wine. He was sure that she was over 28. In fact, he suddenly remembered that she had her 30th birthday in the 'Carrots' and there was a live band. He would need to think through his memories of that evening to see whether it prompted any ideas. Meanwhile, there were emails to read.

There only appeared to be three people in this set of email exchanges, and all their addresses began with the word 'foster'. So one became: 'aunt kath', and then another became '26kath…' How odd to have these numbers, he thought. It then became obvious that the name of '26' was Julie, because of the way she signed herself off. If they were 26 and 28, who were all the other people who were presumably numbered as well? Dave knew that Kath was a 'fosterer' of some sort, and maybe these were the numbers they were known by? It was time to read on.

*

In Lost Whistle, the police due to investigate the murder of Kath Megson were a bit lost themselves. Murder wasn't a crime they actually thought they would have to deal with. Five constables and a sergeant, none with any experience of the fatal offence that had unexpectedly arrived in their world.

The postman had been isolated in a field where sheep were taking a great interest in him, and his bag and its contents. He was isolated because he had handled the envelope that appeared to have killed Kath. All of his other post may have to be destroyed as well, one of the police people told him.

Those Lost Whistle police officers were relieved when the detective inspector arrived from Chrichton and took charge of the situation. She immediately ordered that the postman be brought back from the sheep field, as he should be part of the crime scene. She would be bringing in the forensic team and she was very clear about the rules here. No person without the proper authority should be allowed into the crime scene. They reassured her that nobody unauthorised would get by. The detective inspector had no doubt about that.

A slender and tall lady, probably in her seventies, stopped by, propping her obviously male bicycle up against the telegraph pole. The basket on the front, which had been added and secured using a number of old cut-down waist belts, was adorned with misshapen vegetables, and her wide-brimmed hat with a purple ribbon reminiscent of the suffragette movement clothing of the early 1900s.

"This is so tragic, Danny," she said, addressing the postman.

"It is, Rosemary, but I have to stay on this side of the cordon as I was the last person to see her alive."

Rosemary was wiping tears from her eyes. "I've known Kath most of my life: she lived in the village at her parents' house, same as me, as do many others. I had a lovely husband called Albert, although he died about five years ago. Funnily enough, nobody called him Albert. He was always called Rhubarb because of our surname."

Danny smiled. "It's such a shame, as dear Kath had a new life since that ghastly husband of hers died. He treated those boys appallingly, bullying and threatening them, yet he seemed to treat the girls with great affection on the rare occasion he greeted them. She had barely five months without that beast, and whoever drove the car that killed him did us all a big favour."

The detective inspector was part listening to this as she was dealing with a lot of other issues and wanted to know more. She rushed out to see them but the lady on the bicycle was disappearing along a country lane.

"Who was that?" she barked.

"Are you attempting to talk to me?" Danny asked.

"Why do you have to be so obdurate?" She was clearly fuming.

"If you want to ask me a question then please do. A question will undoubtedly prompt a conversation. That shouldn't involve aggression in any form."

She took some deep breaths and calmed down. She had taken a dislike to Danny and, in her mind, his apparent disrespect for authority.

"Sorry, Danny. I heard you call that person Rosemary. What do you know about her?"

"She lives a couple of lanes away and is a person who works hard to keep the village community together. She has a lovely old 16th-Century house, although I haven't ever been inside it. I've delivered here for over ten years and her husband died about five years ago. To be fair though, my time at any individual house is usually very short."

"Thank you, Danny." Then as she walked away she asked, "What's her surname?"

"Crumble. Rosemary Crumble."

CHAPTER TWO

❖

Steve returned with a pint of beer each for himself and Dave.

"Sorry about the delay, Dave. I had to wait while they changed the barrel."

"No problem. I was deep in thought, to be honest."

"Hmm, anything interesting?" Steve asked as he reflected on just how tall Dave actually was. Steve himself stood at around six feet, yet Dave was notably taller if he stood up straight, which he rarely did. Steve had always presumed this to be a result of him being in a crouched position when driving a train, although maybe a psychologist would come up with a reason. Who knows? Anyway, time to listen.

"It's a project I'm working on related to old train lines. I'd love to write a book about it, but I wouldn't really know where to start. I'll let you know when I've made a bit more progress. Anyway, you were saying about Jen going back and forth to the library. Why is that such an issue?"

"I don't understand why she isn't going there and then returning with a bag full of books. That's what people used to do."

"Maybe she's doing something different there, like some research or something."

"But you can just do that from home."

"Not always. Libraries often have information held on microfiche."

"Micro what?"

"Microfiche. It's a way of storing information by turning it into what amounts to tiny photographs that can be read with a bright light behind them, a bit like an old X-ray display screen in a doctor's consulting room. I imagine there's some way of enlarging the view of them as well. Libraries often use it to store old newspapers so that they don't have to keep them physically, and I'm sure it has many other uses."

"You know there's an entire world out there that I know nothing about. All I really use my computer for is to write emails to customers, and then send them invoices."

"Isn't that all you need it for, though?"

Steve nodded, though before he could speak, a text message appeared on his phone. He looked visibly shocked, and before Dave could ask anything, got his cigarettes out of his jacket pocket and slipped outside.

Dave was left wondering what had happened. He didn't know anything about Steve's family, only that he had grown up locally, and he had a recollection of a brother being mentioned once.

Outside, Steve found Jen blowing smoke rings into the dusk evening.

"Are you okay, Steve? You look very pale, as if you've seen a ghost or something."

Steve smiled and looked at her, the flame from his lighter flickering and showing the beautiful glow of her green eyes.

"Yes. I'm okay, thanks. I just had a bit of unexpected news in a text message from my brother."

"I didn't know you had a brother. Was it good or bad news?"

"Not many people know that I have a brother, and he lives a quiet life on his own without any real desire to see anyone. He says that no-one can be trusted, and he lives in the house I grew up in, a very short distance from here. Mum left everything to him when she died, despite there being two of us, but I think that was an act of guilt."

"Don't you feel bitter about that?"

"Not really. He was fostered for a good while after my dad died as my mum felt that she could only look after one of us. I'm pretty sure that's worth feeling bitter about. He always viewed me as the chosen one, and I don't blame him for that."

"What was the message all about, if you don't mind me asking?"

Steve decided not to tell her the whole message.

"It was that his foster aunt, as he called her, has been murdered."

"Oh my goodness, how awful. Did she live far away?"

"It was a funny little place and must be about fifty miles away. You probably won't know it: Lost Whistle." At this point Jen almost choked on her glass of rosé. "Is everything okay?"

"Yes," she said croakily. "I think I just need to pop to the toilet."

Steve was even more bemused now. Jen had clearly reacted to hearing 'Lost Whistle', but why? What would it mean to her? He walked back inside the 'Carrots' to re-join Dave.

"Are you okay, Steve?"

"Do you know, Dave, I'm not sure. While I was outside I told Jen about the text message, which was from my brother, by the way…"

"I didn't know you had a brother."

"I'll come to that. Now, where was I? Oh, yes, and I didn't read her all of it. Calm down, Dave, I'll let you ask questions shortly. I don't quite understand the second part of the message yet myself."

"So, what was the first part about?"

Here we go again, thought Steve.

"To give you a bit of background – when my dad died my mum couldn't cope with two of us, so Eddie was sent away to be fostered. Not a time that he talks fondly of, if indeed you can get him to talk about it at all. When Mum died she left everything to him so he's now living in what was the family home. Anyway, his text message was telling me that his 'foster aunt', as he called her, has been murdered."

"That's very sad. Was she local?"

"No, it was a tiny place about fifty miles away. It's called 'Lost Whistle'."

Dave nearly choked on his beer and Steve was now even more confused. Why would Jen and Dave both seem to know Lost Whistle?

"So what do you know about Lost Whistle?"

Dave had to think on his feet.

"When you're a train driver it's the kind of place that you look for. Having your photo taken by the village name and searching for any remnants of a station that was there before Dr Beeching's team were. What was wrong with the message that you decided not to tell Jen? I'm sure it would be of no consequence to her."

"I don't know, really; I just didn't want to reveal a flaw in my world because I want to impress her and be with her so much."

"Maybe being completely honest with her will help you to develop a relationship. What was the second part of the message, if you don't mind me asking?"

"It should have been him."

CHAPTER THREE

❖

In Lost Whistle, the police were itching to get on with their investigation inside the house and could see that the forensic team were starting to clear up after their work.

"Can I be on my way now, please?" asked Danny the postman.

The stern detective inspector said he could, but that she needed his address.

Danny was immediately on his bike and called back, "I live over there." He looked over his shoulder, smiling at the DI, who looked at her sergeant with bluster in her eyes.

"Bloody locals. I'm already sure they know more than they're telling us."

Danny cycled to Rosemary's house.

"I'm not keen on that detective inspector."

"Neither am I, young Danny. She wants to know more than is necessary for her to know. I suggest that we answer the questions we need to and then let her work out what else she wants to know."

Danny nodded his agreement; he'd like Lost Whistle to be the enigma it had always been. He believed that he could be hidden away here.

DI Rachel Hawley was deeply suspicious about all of the villagers, even the local police. They seemed reticent to be engaged in conversation. Was there something that shouldn't be revealed?

Kath's body was now on its way to the mortuary for examination and the house was declared ready for investigation. DI Hawley was straight in there with her sergeant in tow, while the local police were positioned to stop anyone entering.

As Danny continued with his delivery he was constantly being asked about Kath's death.

"Actually, it's a murder." The number of times he repeated those words that morning was not surprising as the news was spreading. What was also spreading was Danny's sense of shock at the suddenness of her demise. He had known Kath for a long time now, and he needed to stop and let his girlfriend know as she had been very close to her at various times. Having been there at the tragic moment, he had a brief celebrity status in the village, and news had also found its way to the town of Chrichton where a journalist from the newspaper for the county had decided it could be useful to have a conversation with the Lost Whistle postman as well.

In Fenningwood, Dave and Steve were puzzling over what 'it should have been him' actually meant. Dave was keen to get to the library to use a computer there to try and find out more, but that would have to wait until tomorrow. Jen needed to get in touch with 26kath (Julie) to find out what she knew about Kath's death. She had become detached from the conversation in the pub and was looking for ways to make her excuses and leave. Should she break her own rule and send a message from her laptop at home? Maybe the wine was making her more relaxed about this self-imposed rule, which was only there because she felt shame about having been fostered. She decided that she would use her own laptop.

On the walk home, Jen was wondering whether Julie would still be awake. She did have an 'emergency' number for her, and if this wasn't an emergency then what was? Jen also had a compelling urge to look at the phone that Aunt Kath had sent her. Maybe there could be some voyage of discovery there after all.

She got home and poured herself another glass of rosé. Should she look at the phone or call Julie first? As it was 9:30 in the evening she thought she had better contact Julie first. While her laptop was starting up, she put the phone Aunt Kath had sent her on to charge. She wondered what this evening would unveil. As much as Kath's husband made her, and all the other girls, feel ill at ease, it had always sounded a lot worse in the boys' rooms of the foster home. She always loved its name: Quilter's End. A very fitting name for a house so full of patchwork and quilts homemade by Aunt Kath. Her husband was a very distant man who liked to be called 'Sir.' Kath had sometimes wondered whether it was really just an accident that had killed him, or was it something more sinister?

In Kath's house, DI Hawley was wondering exactly the same thing, and although it was getting dark, her search of Quilter's End would continue for a while longer before resuming in the morning. She fully understood the name of the house now, as there were patchwork quilts everywhere: all of the sofas had them draped across, as did all the beds, and there were two beds in many of the eight bedrooms. Even the dining room chair cushions and napkins had a patchwork ornateness about them. But one sofa was bare! It puzzled DI Hawley. Should there have been a quilt on that sofa as well, and if so, where could it have gone, and was it relevant in any way?

CHAPTER FOUR

❖

In Fenningwood, Jen was about to phone Julie. The phone at the other end rang, but there was no answer. She hadn't planned for that! An impersonal voicemail recording invited her to leave a message, but she just pressed the 'end' icon, feeling completely deflated. She hadn't realised how much she had built herself up to that moment and felt emotionally drained. It would have to be email after all, then. Jen sat and looked around her flat for a few moments. It was spartan, in that she didn't have any comforts around. There certainly weren't any family photos: what family did she have? She didn't have anything related to her mum, who had effectively disappeared from Jen's life when she was twelve years old, although they had lived together in a social housing flat in East Fenningwood. 'The rough end of town' as she would learn in adult life that the locals called it. She got herself ready for school as her mum was usually in bed. Jen was careful not to step on the used syringes that littered their flat. She needed a break from her thoughts.

Her laptop had started up now but then she realised she didn't have her Quilter's End email address stored as it was on the library computer. She tried many ways to bring it to life but she just couldn't work it out. She needed someone with some practical knowledge, or 'savvy' as they called it at work. The only people she could think of were Steve and Dave. But could she trust them? Tonight, she would have to. Jen gave it a second thought, and then a third thought. If she told them about her background, the 'virtual' security wall that she believed she had built around her would be broken, potentially leaving her emotions exposed. Something she had never allowed since leaving foster care for adulthood fourteen years ago. For a few moments Jen just wept, tears running down her face and dark blobs of wetness landing on her green silk top. She reached for her phone again.

"Steve, I need you to come over, and can you bring Dave as well, please? Oh, and please don't come empty-handed!"

"Of course, Jen. We're on our way." Steve relayed the message to Dave, who started to get his rucksack that he always carried with him, and he was ready to pop to the late shop a couple of doors along from 'The Carrots'. "Something is definitely not right with Jen."

"Let's see what we can do to help her, Steve." Dave was worried about accidentally revealing what he knew; he would have to keep his wits about him.

Jen was delighted to see them both and hugged Steve like (he felt) she had never hugged him before. Her head momentarily rested on his shoulder, and she noticed one of her tears on his top as well.

"Why are you crying?" Steve asked. Jen smiled and he could see the wetness of tears settled in the bottom of her beautiful green eyes. There were also a couple of giveaway tear lines that expressed her feelings on her light brown skin.

"Thank you for coming over, both of you. Let me explain what I need to do, and to be honest, I'm going to open up to you."

Dave nodded and Steve filled their glasses quietly. The floor was Jen's.

"I want to talk about Lost Whistle."

Dave discreetly adjusted himself on the footstall, trying to remember his story about train drivers wanting to go there. Steve was now intrigued as he knew that his brother, although he hadn't seen him for years and didn't really have anything to do with him, had been fostered in Lost Whistle for a while. Why on earth would Jen want to talk about the place?

"You probably need to know a bit about my past, so here we go. I grew up in East Fenningwood. My mum was a drug addict and I never knew my dad. Given the colour of my skin I assume he was a black man. Where did she meet him and how did I occur? I don't mind what the answer is, I just wonder about who he is. Sorry, boys, I'm rambling."

They both sat agog, awaiting Jen's next words.

"When I was twelve, Mum didn't come home, and I didn't know what to do. I was able to look after myself but I didn't want to be alone. I walked from East Fenningwood into the 'posh' part of town and looked completely out of place. A mixed-race girl bordering on her teenage years looking for help. A police car happened to pass by and then stop. They weren't sure about me, they said. In reality there wasn't anyone more unsure about me than I was. They took me home and although they didn't say as much, they were appalled. I ended up at the police station until Social Services arrived. I hated that feeling of suddenly being reliant but…"

"You were twelve years old: a kid; surely you were reliant on someone?"

"No I wasn't, Dave. I was on my own and—"

"Surely grandparents or aunts and uncles stepped in?"

"No. All of them disowned Mum when they found out that her baby was fathered by a black man. You both know what Fenningwood is like. People talk about 'no barriers', but in the end I felt that I was out of place. Not now, though: I hold my head high.

"Back to what I was saying. Mum's purse was always available so I could buy food and fend for myself. I didn't realise the mess that I was living in until it was pointed out to me: the unmade bed that we shared, though only when she actually came home; the mould on the walls, although to be honest it was always there and I didn't know what mould was so it just seemed normal. Then they asked about the syringes. I just said, 'Oh, they're Mum's,' as that's what I had always known. The two people from Social Services, having jotted down lots of notes, were clearly wondering what to do with me.

"The policewoman who was with them, who obviously wasn't used to this kind of issue, looked astonished at what my reality was. Then I was asked a question: *'Where is your dad?'* I told them that I didn't know as I hadn't ever met him. I think I was fifteen and sitting in my patchwork-covered bed at the foster home when a question popped into my head. Does my dad know that I exist?

"Back at the scene, as it was, having at twelve years old revealed that I didn't know this piece of information, it seemed to be their final call to action. Before I knew it, I was sitting in a police car being whisked away to the station. Sorry, boys. I'm really rambling on."

"Don't be sorry at all," said Steve. "I think you may be helping me to understand my brother a little bit more, because he did have a spell in prison, though I don't know why. So, what happened at the police station?"

"They looked after me while Social Services organised a place for me to stay that night. The police were very kind and even went back to the flat to get my favourite teddy and blanket. Having them made me feel so much better." Once again, her green eyes glistened, and not because of a new flame; this time, there were teardrops forming.

"From there, I was sent to a foster home in a place called Lost Whistle."

A penny suddenly dropped for Steve. "That's where my brother Eddie was sent to a foster home as well. Quilter's End, it was called. Apparently there was a violent man who made them call him 'Sir' and Eddie hated that."

Jen's tears started to flow again. "I was there too, Steve. There were three girls and three boys at a time, though we weren't allowed to mix; even our mealtimes were different! Aunt Kath, our foster carer, was lovely, but her husband, who I didn't meet very often at all in the six years that I was there, was reputed to be a horrible man. Kath was always making patchwork quilts, hence the name of the house. The quilts were everywhere; her dream was to have all the sofas and chairs covered in her own work one day. I wonder if she ever achieved that.

"To be honest, Steve, if Eddie had been there when I was, I wouldn't have known him anyway as the boys went to their school, and we went to the girls' school. That's another story!"

Jen suddenly remembered that she hadn't sent an email to Julie.

*

Detective Inspector Hawley was still at Chrichton Police Station sitting in a room that, although dark, was lit up by a powerful desk lamp. As she was writing notes to try and work out the Lost Whistle murder – or was it murders, as her copper's nose was suggesting to her? – shadows were cast around the room by her every movement.

Why would the letter be sent to a man – although she didn't actually check the recipient's name – who had died five months ago? Who would want to kill him? Based on what Rosemary Crumble said, he wasn't a very pleasant man at all. But could her word be trusted? DI Hawley had no idea at this stage. A car accident in a small village had killed him when he was knocked over, and she had investigated it. She was doubting her findings and needed to find out more about that, as well as why she lived in what sounded like a very large house. Quilter's End needed a thorough search to establish everything that she could. That's where she would start tomorrow morning. For now, she just needed some sleep.

*

Back in Fenningwood, Jen finally got around to what she had asked Steve and Dave to help with.

"Now you know the background of what happened to me, I need to ask you a favour. I would like to email my friend Julie, who I was in the home with, but I can't remember the email address. Can either of you help, please?"

Dave was acutely aware that he had to be incredibly careful here, as he knew Jen's email address and password without having to look them up. He decided to ask questions.

"Can you remember anything about it, Jen?"

"I remember the word 'foster' at the beginning, and then I think it may have been my number but—"

"Your number?!" interjected Steve.

"Yes, I was number 28."

Steve looked shocked and was clearly pondering something. "Presumably you've emailed her before, so I don't really understand why her email address wouldn't 'pop up' for you. I'm really puzzled, Jen."

"It's probably because I have always used the library computers to contact Julie or Aunt Kath. So, is that why you go there so often? I did wonder as I hadn't ever seen you carrying any books. Dave, you go there too, for the computers. You must see each other."

Jen smiled: her somewhat secret world was being unravelled in front of her own eyes.

Dave gave a nervous cough and tried to move the focus away from him. "Can we get back to the business at hand, please?"

Steve and Jen looked at each other and giggled for no apparent reason.

"Sorry," they both said in unison.

Dave continued. "So far we have foster 28. Is there any more that you can think of?"

Jen shook her head.

"Let's type in what you have and see what comes up." Dave was feeling anxious as he knew the answer to his own question but had to resist the temptation to help too much. Her suggestion was rejected. Jen looked frustrated. "What was the foster lady's name? Would that be part of it?"

Then Steve joined in.

"You're very good at this, Dave; it's almost as if you know what's going to happen."

Dave had to 'think on his feet' again.

"Not at all, Steve, I just happened to have helped people before. It's usually only logic that gets you there."

"There it is, Dave – you were correct. When I added Kath and then the Lost Whistle website it turned up."

"Jot it down quickly, then when you remember your password you can jot that down too. Just keep them somewhere safe."

"Now I have the email address I can remember the password. Thank you so much."

"No problem, Jen, but now I need to be on my way. Are you coming, Steve?" He sensed that Jen wanted to be alone.

"I'm on my way with you, Dave."

Jen thanked them for their help. It was too late to contact Julie and she felt emotionally exhausted. She collapsed into bed with her teddy and blanket in her hands.

CHAPTER FIVE

❧

George Hicks woke early, as he had heard there had been a murder in Lost Whistle the previous day. Nothing had been reported anywhere, although he had overheard a whisper in his local pub just outside of Chrichton, where he lived. George was the chief journalist for the *Chrichton and District Examiner*, having spent forty years on national newspapers and earning himself the nickname 'Hick-hack'. He was well respected in his industry and reputed to have amazing 'news sense', enabling him to get to the bottom of stories better and faster than most of his colleagues. George sensed a story here and decided to take a drive to Lost Whistle, to see what he could find out for himself.

Detective Inspector Hawley was on her way to Lost Whistle as well. There were people she needed to talk to, starting with Danny and Rosemary. She was suspicious about both of them for some reason, but she needed to have another good look around Kath Megson's house first. She would be joined by her sergeant: Tomi Baker.

Danny was getting ready to start his round of deliveries. Nearly all of his colleagues delivered using a van of some sort, but he had to use a bicycle. He often wondered why and decided to ask his manager.

"History, Danny. History. Yours, not ours. Oh, and try not to murder anyone today." The fat manager laughed at his appallingly insensitive joke.

Danny walked away, loaded himself up and cycled away. An anger was building inside of him. He pedalled furiously that morning, and after a good while he had calmed down, with help from the lovely greetings he received from his customers. He was still being asked about the murder but got on his way and turned the corner towards what had been Kath's house. The corner was one part of a grassed triangle as part of the road junction, and in the middle of that triangle was a beautiful apple blossom tree, and one other that he didn't know the name of... Then Danny saw DI Hawley.

"Hello, Mrs Policewoman," Danny said almost disdainfully.

She winced and then spoke. "You can call me DI Hawley."

He found himself back in the anger mode he had left behind only an hour or so ago with his manager, but before he could respond, a new voice suddenly appeared.

"Hello, Rachel. How are you? Bullying and looking down on a postman, I see."

DI Hawley was seething when George the journalist asked her the question. She turned and looked at him venomously. "Who the hell do you think that you are, calling me Rachel? Can't you please show some respect?"

DI Hawley, some thirty years younger than George, was red in the face by now, and then Danny joined in. "Do you always wail at people on the first occasion you see them? You certainly did with me."

"What the hell has it got to do with you?"

"I rest my case, as you lot say." George winked at Danny and by this time, DI Hawley looked like a tomato that was ready to explode. "You're obviously stressed then, Rachel, but as you well know, I can often get information that could be helpful to your investigation, and you just can't get it because your approach makes people clam up."

She looked at George with annoyance in her eyes. Danny was amused by the exchange, and DI Hawley turned to him. "I need to talk to you, Danny, and it's a matter of urgency."

"I'll be finished in a couple of hours. Where shall I meet you?"

"I wanted to see you now!"

"I'm not authorised to stop delivering mail, so you would have to talk to my manager."

She sighed at what she saw as an unnecessary obstacle. Summoning politeness out of frustration, she started again.

"Okay, what's his name and phone number?"

"I have the phone number but I'm just trying to remember his name."

"How can you possibly not remember his name?"

"In this industry people are often known by nicknames. I was told his real name when I started but that was some time ago."

"A bit like me being known as 'Hick-hack'."

"Haven't you got better things to do, George?" A sinking feeling came over DI Hawley. "Back to you, Danny. Let's just leave it until you've finished. Can you meet me at Quilter's End in two hours?"

"That should be okay."

"I could do with a chat as well, please, Danny."

"I'll meet you in the 'Drunken Duck' half an hour later, George." Danny was pleased that he now had thinking time in case any awkward questions were asked.

Danny cycled on; George took a walk around the village to see if he could find someone to talk to about what had happened. Maybe there would be someone in the small church who could help him. DI Hawley went into Quilter's End with Tomi to undertake a more detailed inspection.

In Fenningwood, Jen was coming up to a break between appointments and decided to phone Julie. It was to be a revelation!

CHAPTER SIX

❖

Julie had expected the call from Jen, who was sitting on a bench outside 'The Bunch of Carrots'. After the initial pleasantries, Jen asked the question.

"What actually happened?"

"Kath died yesterday by a letter that was delivered to her, though in fact was addressed to her late husband. It's over five months since he died after being in an accident with a car. The postman who delivered the letter is my boyfriend, Danny, so he saw Kath collapse and die in front of him."

"Gosh, how traumatic: is he okay?"

"He seems to be, he's just getting on with his job. I don't know a huge amount about him yet other than he's been a postman for a good while and that he's three months older than me. Some strange things have happened at Kath's in the last six months. She had finished the quilts to cover all her furniture, as I'm sure you'll remember she always wanted to."

"Mmm, yes, I do."

"One went missing mysteriously and no-one ever found out where it had disappeared to."

"How did you know about it?"

"I'd popped round to see her one day and noticed that it wasn't on the sofa it usually adorned. I asked Kath whether it was being washed and she told me it had suddenly disappeared one day." Jen thought that was very odd in a place like Lost Whistle, especially when there were so many expensive things in Kath's house.

"She had that friend; Rosemary, I think her name was…"

"That's right."

"...Would she know?"

"Apparently not, but who does know? One day it may turn up."

"What about you and Danny? How did you get together?"

"As you know, I've lived in Lost Whistle since we left Kath's fourteen years ago. I only have a small two-bedroomed cottage that I own but it's enough for me. Back to your question. I was in the Drunken Duck one night..."

"Gosh, I'd forgotten all about that place. Sorry to change the subject for a moment but have you any photos of Quilter's End?"

"I have one in the snow I think I can send you."

"Thank you. You were talking about being in the Drunken Duck..."

"...Well, Danny came in. He used to live in Chrichton, where we went to school. We got talking and we've had quite a few dates since that night. I'm not sure it will come to anything, which is a lot about me not letting my guard down, I suppose."

"I'm exactly the same, Julie. Would you like me to come over and see you? I could be there in a couple of hours or so."

"You don't need to, although that is very kind. There's something I need to tell you."

"That sounds intriguing!"

"Well, we are the two sole beneficiaries of Kath's will. That is, you and me."

Jen fell silent.

"Are you still there, Jen?"

"Yes, sorry. I was just absorbing that piece of information."

"That's understandable..."

"...But how do you know that?"

"Kath told me, and when I went to the solicitors with her, they confirmed it. At some point I will have to get your address, Jen."

"Just let me know when you need it."

"It's only really the house and its contents, although the house alone is worth over two million pounds."

"TWO MILLION POUNDS!" Jen blurted out, suddenly aware that others sitting outside The Carrots were now staring at her. She smiled and waved at them as if to say that everything was just fine. "Two million pounds?" she whispered to Julie.

"Where are you, Jen?"

"I'm sitting outside our local pub and, actually, I need to get back to work. Can I call you later?"

"Yes, of course. I'll speak to you then."

*

In Lost Whistle, George was sitting outside the local pub as well. The strangely named 'Drunken Duck'. He was thinking about how to approach this piece of investigative journalism and making some notes when he saw a lady on a bicycle coming along the road. He stood up and doffed his fedora hat.

"Good morning, madam."

She pulled over and wished the stranger good morning, too. "You're early at the pub, young man."

George couldn't remember the last time he had been called 'young man'.

"Well, thank you. I'm George Hicks from the *Chrichton and District Examiner* and I'm just finding out what I can about the murder that has taken place."

"Oh! Dreadful affair. Poor Kath…"

"You knew her, then?"

"We had been lifelong friends and—"

"Sorry, I didn't catch your name."

"Rosemary. Rosemary Crumble."

"What a lovely name."

"My dear late husband hated it as he spent so much of his life being called Rhubarb!"

George was trying not to snigger so he faked a sneeze as Rosemary sat down at the table.

"How very unusual."

"I'm sorry, you've lost me."

"One solitary sneeze; they usually come in twos or threes."

At that moment, George realised that Rosemary wasn't a woman to be taken in by anything: she could see right through him.

"You must be very upset about your friend. Do you know anything about the murder?"

"Poor Kath. Such a dear friend and when her ghastly husband died in a car accident about five months ago, I thought she was finally freed from that monster."

"These are very strong and what feels like bitter words about Mr… I'm sorry, I don't know his name."

"Megson was their surname, but he always wanted to be called 'Sir' and he wasn't a knight or anything like it, just someone who was a nasty bully. Those poor kids." She paused. "Dozens of them…"

"Dozens?!" exclaimed George.

"They were foster parents. He was in charge of the boys, and Kath looked after the girls."

"I'm glad we've cleared that up. Do you know anything about her death?"

"Danny, you know him, the post boy. He told me that the letter was addressed to Kath's husband. She opened the envelope but the letter inside was sealed in some way, so she went to get some scissors. She had scissors everywhere, you know; when you spend the amount of time that she did quilting or sewing, I suppose it's just an occupational hazard."

"That's interesting. I'd like to come back to that and—"

"Yes, all in good time, George. Danny said Kath cut open the seal, some powder puffed out and she just keeled over. He had immediately taken a few steps back as he didn't want to be at any risk."

"What a horrible experience for him, and such a horrible thing to witness. I have another couple of questions that I'd like to ask, but I feel as if I'm holding you up."

"Don't worry. It was George, wasn't it?" He nodded. "What are they, then?"

"You mentioned Kath's husband, and if I may say so, in quite virulent terms, also that he died in a car accident. Can you enlighten me about those a bit more at all?"

"Kath's husband, who was actually named Robert, despite insisting that people called him 'Sir', was very pompous and, as I said before: a bully."

"In what way?"

"When they were fostering they would usually have three girls and three boys. Kath looked after the girls and Robert was in charge of the boys—"

"Sorry to interrupt, but you said that Kath 'looked after' and Robert was 'in charge of.' They are two quite different descriptions."

"It will become clear, I hope, as I explain things. The kids weren't allowed to mix. I'll give you examples. The boys and girls had different mealtimes. They weren't allowed to play on the village triangle together; it was an hour for the boys and then an hour for the girls."

"But surely Kath was complicit in that?"

"Kath lived her married life in fear of Robert and indulged herself in her hobbies. That's why if you go into the house, you will see patchwork quilts everywhere. If she dared to question him, she was scared that she would suffer the same fate as those boys."

"What do you mean by that?"

"They were beaten by him. If I walked or cycled past in the evening, I could hear their screams. It was awful."

"But these were children trying to escape from a bad life…"

"I know, George, but there are some people who get self-gratification from hurting others, and thereby feel powerful."

"What about the car accident, then?"

"He was a pedestrian on Lost Whistle Lane, which is just off Pea Lane, the main road from Chrichton, usually a very quiet and slow road, but a car obviously hit him with some force into the ditch at the side of the road and he was found dead there in the morning."

"Goodness. He must have had horrible injuries?"

"Strangely, he didn't."

That comment sent George's mind racing.

"How did Kath not know that he was missing?"

"They lived very separate lives. She would use the front door and he used a side door. She didn't know until she rang the clanging bell to let him know that breakfast was ready…"

"Rang the clanging bell?!"

"…That was his way; he wanted everyone to be subservient to him."

"Rosemary, it has been a delight to talk to you and thank you so much. If I would like to, can I contact you again, please? And how would I do that?"

"Just drop by. If my bicycle is there I'm most likely to be at home. I'm on the corner just into Fipple Lane and the house is called 'Witch's Wash'."

George shuddered at the name and decided he would ask about that another time.

"Thank you again, Rosemary, and I look forward to talking to you again."

"It will be my pleasure, George, and do feel free to drop by."

George was left pondering such a lot of information, and there had been two deaths that he was puzzled about. Kath had certainly been murdered, but was Robert's death really an accident? He needed to know more.

CHAPTER SEVEN

❖

In Fenningwood, Dave was so intrigued by what was going on, he was actually thinking about buying himself a laptop. It was a bright morning, and he knew that if he made an order early enough, he would be able to collect it fairly locally later that day. When the library opened he would be placing his order and then investigating Steve's brother.

It was Jen's day off also and she wanted to spend some time reflecting, though she also fancied going out for lunch and gave Steve an early-morning call. He agreed to meet her at one o'clock. Jen had five hours to deal with things on her mind, and then an hour to get showered and ready to meet Steve. She decided to start with Kath's phone.

Starting with Kath's text messages, she saw that there were a lot between her and a man called Robert, and some of them were quite combative. In one message she said, 'you won't die a natural death.' Jen shuddered and then noticed that this message was only six months old. After reading a few more, she realised that Robert was Kath's husband, who had died just five months ago. At Kath's, when being fostered, Jen had only known him as 'Sir' and just for a moment wondered whether his death had been an accident. Surely Kath couldn't have killed him. She certainly didn't want to believe that.

Dave, meanwhile, was impatient to make his purchase and the library didn't open for a couple of hours yet, so he called Steve, who was bemused at getting two calls before 7:15 in the morning.

"Hello, Dave."

"Hello, mate. Sorry to bother you but can I pop round and use your computer for ten minutes?"

"Yes, of course. I'm going to work at 8 o'clock. What's the rush?"

"I've decided to buy a laptop and if I order it early I can pick it up not far away this afternoon."

"It's going to be a busy day as Jen fancied going to 'The Carrots' for lunch."

"I may see you there but in any case I'll be round in a few minutes, and thank you."

"You're welcome, mate."

There wasn't much else of interest to Jen on Kath's phone, although for a reason that she didn't really understand, it made her think about her mum, and then her dad. She was wondering where her mum could be. Was she still in the flat in East Fenningwood? Would they ever meet again? Then a dark thought crossed her mind: was she still alive? She didn't really know how to find out. Maybe she should walk to East Fenningwood.

Jen then thought about her dad. What was his name? How could she ever find him? Where did he live? Her questions were endless. He may have walked through Fenningwood but she would never have known. Was he into drugs like her mum was? She decided to shower and think about her next move.

*

In Lost Whistle, DI Hawley hadn't got very far with Danny yesterday. She had found him irritating and elusive to the point that she had even missed basics question such as, 'what is your surname?' George the journalist, meanwhile, had enjoyed an enlightening conversation with Danny that previous day. He was now sitting in his office, starting to piece a story together.

DI Hawley saw Rosemary cycling by.

"Excuse me, madam, can I ask you a question?"

"Please wouldn't have gone amiss, but go ahead and be brief. I have a Parish Council meeting to attend."

"It's very short. I was wondering if you could let me know what Danny's surname is – please?"

"It's interesting that you ask: I'm not sure that I know. Good day."

"I'll bet that she does, Tomi. What are they all hiding?"

George decided to return to Lost Whistle, but not until he had investigated Danny a bit further. He had discovered Danny's surname and so remained a step ahead of DI Hawley. He would love to visit Quilter's End, though wouldn't ever be let in by the police. Maybe Rosemary had a key, he thought. In the meantime, the information about Danny was a revelation, especially about his time in prison and his two main associates in crime, not that he recognised their names at all. George decided to keep this information to himself for the time being.

DI Hawley's officers had gone through everything at Quilter's End as they looked for evidence, but they hadn't found anything yet. The investigation hadn't got off to a good start.

*

In Fenningwood, Dave went to Steve's flat and after a quick perusal of available laptops, made his choice and paid. It would be in stock where he wanted it, that afternoon. He thanked Steve and returned home very happy.

Jen was showered and decided that she would take a walk to East Fenningwood to talk to her mum for the first time in twenty years. She didn't know why, it was just an inner compulsion. She decided to dress casually in jeans and a T-shirt: she didn't want to look out of place. Just after 8 o'clock, Steve drove past her walking along and wondered where she was off to. The library wasn't open yet and she hadn't stopped at Snow and Co. He guessed he would probably find out at lunchtime – well, maybe.

Jen carried on walking, and it wasn't an arduous walk at all, but her heart was pounding as she was going to the place she had last left in a police car twenty years earlier. After she left the roads with detached houses, she walked through the narrow lane that went through what actually was Fenning Wood and arrived at the estate where she had grown up, until the age of twelve anyway. It was like stepping into a different world that she had either forgotten, or maybe didn't notice when she was young, because she hadn't known anything different at the time. Her school was on the edge of the wood and nobody ever seemed to go into the town. The convenience store on the estate stocked everything they had ever needed.

She took a deep breath to avoid crying. It had been an emotional couple of days. Jen then moved towards Block Three, the three-storey building she had lived in. They weren't allowed to be higher than the trees of the wood, she now knew, and in that way they were hidden from the affluence of the town. She went to the door of the ground-floor flat where she had lived with her mum two decades ago, paused for several moments to gather her thoughts and then knocked on the door. Her heart was pounding. The person who answered the door definitely wasn't her mother.

"Hello, how can I help you?"

"Oh, hello, I was looking for Laura Greening." Her voice a bit shaky.

"Okay. Who are you, if you don't mind me asking?"

"I'm her daughter, Jennifer. Why do you ask?"

"Do you have some proof of identification?"

"Proof of ID? What's going on?"

"I need it before I can tell you any further information."

Jen, feeling frustrated and bemused, produced her driving licence.

"And who are you?"

After checking Jen's identification, she went on.

"I'm here on behalf of Social Services trying to sort out Laura Greening's affairs, as she died three weeks ago." Jen's eyes filled with tears. "If you have any further questions, I'll give you the name and number of the person to speak to."

"But I need to—"

"I'm sorry, but I can't tell you any more than I know and have told you. I suggest that you call Janice."

It was a name that sounded familiar to Jen, and as she walked away she called out kindly, "Thank you. I understand your position."

Before walking through the narrow lane in Fenning Wood she sat on a bench and watched some toddlers being helped along, walking and running with their young mums. She had played on that very same grass area as a young girl and had as much fun as these kids were having now. However, she needed to get back home and phone Janice.

*

Dave was in a quandary about what to do. Should he go to the library to see if there had been an email exchange, or should he go and see whether his laptop had arrived? He decided he would do the latter and soon set off for the train ride to the town where he could collect it. He would pop into a tea shop and then have a look around as he hadn't been there for a fair while.

DI Hawley was in a quandary as well. The search of Quilter's End had thrown up no evidence apart from the one missing quilt. While she waited for results from the forensic team, she decided to start her team on house-to-house enquiries while she interviewed Rosemary. But where exactly did Rosemary live? All Danny had said was that it was a couple of lanes away, but that could be in any direction.

After briefing the team on the enquiry requirements, she set off on foot to find Rosemary's house. Surely it couldn't be very far away. On the other side of the green from Quilter's End was the pub, The Drunken Duck. *What a peculiar name*, she thought. Rosemary always seemed to appear from the left as she looked at it, so that was the way she would go.

Before the police started the house-to-house work, Sergeant Tomi Baker called them all together to thank them for their work to date.

"Thank you, Sarge. *You* have our respect." It was a poignant comment.

*

In Fenningwood, Steve was working at speed to be finished by 12:30 to be showered and ready to meet Jen half an hour later. Dave was happily sitting on the train, or 'his office' as he liked to call it. Jen was about to walk through the trees. She waved back at the kids and mums.

"I'll be back," she called out, tears now flowing down her face. She had decided that if she was about to inherit a million pounds or more, the people who lived where she spent the first twelve years of her life would benefit too. She knew what it was like to live a life, 'behind the trees.'

CHAPTER EIGHT

❧

Danny had received an unexpected text message from Eddie Pitcher, someone he had met in prison. He knew Eddie had spent some time in Lost Whistle, but still, the message surprised him. It read simply, 'It should have been him at Quilter's End.' He obviously didn't know about Kath's husband, though he did know about Kath dying. How could he possibly know about it? There hadn't been any news coverage to date, so how was he getting his information? Danny felt angry and decided that he would drive to see Eddie. He knew he was pretty much a recluse these days. He did have his address somewhere, then suddenly remembered it was in a place called Fenningwood, and that was only about fifty miles away. That was his task for the afternoon.

DI Hawley found what she thought was Rosemary's house but there was no bicycle outside. Then she remembered Rosemary had said she was off to a Parish Council meeting, and how long that would last was anyone's guess.

*

Jen got home feeling a bit of an emotional wreck, though she knew she had to phone this Janice. She braced herself, grabbed a glass of water and sat down.

"Hello, Social Services."

"Oh, hello, um, can I speak to Janice, please?"

"This is Janice. How can I help you?"

"My name is Jennifer Greening and—"

"Jen, how lovely to hear your voice again. It must be, what? Twenty years? I was the person who came with the police to collect you from East Fenningwood."

Jen could hold on no longer and burst into tears.

"Let it all out, Jen. You still have a lot to recover from, even though many years have passed. The memories and emotional pain don't really leave you."

"Thanks, Janice. I've calmed down a bit now."

"I'm guessing you've been to the flat where you lived with your mum?"

"Yes." Jen stopped to blow her nose and wipe her eyes and took a big glug of water. "I didn't really expect her to be dead at such a young age, if I'm honest."

"This is going to sound brutal, Jen, but it was one syringe too far. Would you like me to come over?"

"I'm supposed to be going out for lunch at one o'clock..."

"It isn't eleven o'clock yet and I can be in Fenningwood in ten minutes."

"But what about your other work?"

"That can wait an hour, and your case has always been close to my heart. I'll see you very shortly. I just need your address."

Jen sat back in the chair and sighed. She felt exhausted even though she had only been awake for a few hours. The sigh she gave was enormous, and she suddenly realised with an overwhelming sense of loneliness that she now didn't know a single blood relative.

*

George Hicks had learned quite a lot about Danny's time in prison, and now also a little bit about others he had spent and served time with. It turned out that Danny had been jailed for car theft and arson, somebody called Eddie Pitcher was there for similar crimes, and a third person called George Williams, who had been convicted of supplying class-A drugs. They all seemed to have been released, and George wondered where and how he could track them all down. The hairs on the back of his neck suggested that 'Hick-hack' was back!

*

DI Hawley was wondering what to do. No information that she

didn't already know had been forthcoming from the house-to-house searches. She decided to return to Chrichton to move the forensic team along. First of all, she had to find Tomi Baker.

"I'm going back to Chrichton to hassle forensics. You can let uniform go when they've finished. You need to stay here to find Rosemary and Danny when they go past. I still don't know Danny's surname, and they both need to be asked a lot of questions. Got it?"

"Please wouldn't have gone amiss," Tomi said with a wry smile.

"Don't you bloody start. I've had enough with that Crumble woman and the postman who is like the elusive butterfly. I'll be back to pick you up later."

"Okay, ma'am." And with that, DI Hawley raced off. Tomi suddenly realised how easy it would have been to kill someone on these lanes. Deliberately or otherwise. Why hadn't Kath's husband had any impact injuries? It was puzzling her.

She gathered the officers together and once again thanked them for their efforts, and off they went. Tomi was alone in a tiny village, sitting on the bench on the green, watching three young mums helping their toddlers learn to walk and run. She enjoyed the scene, not knowing that someone fifty miles away had just witnessed a similar event, and that she had spent six years at Quilter's End.

*

Danny was racing around his delivery on this day, as he wanted to finish and get on his way to see Eddie in Fenningwood. He was angry because he believed that Eddie had killed Kath. He had liked her, and was in the mood to confront him.

*

Jen heard the knock on her door and it was Janice. Yes, she was twenty years older, but then so was Jen, though the warmth in her smile and the softness of her voice took Jen back all of those twenty years to that same person who had rescued her, and also organised a new life for her at Quilter's End.

She almost fell into Janice's arms, sobbing, unlike the twelve-year-old that Janice had known and at that time seemed incapable of emotion. Jen had learned a lot from Kath.

"It must have been an emotional day, Jen."

"It has been a strange few days, to be honest: I found out that my foster carer Kath had died; then I found out that the brother of one of my closest friends was also fostered there; and then I found out that my mum died. It's been a lot to take in."

Janice could only begin to imagine how Jen felt and told her so.

"I'm delighted to see you seem to have settled."

"The truth is, I'm settled in some ways but not others. I have a decent job, I have a nice flat and I have a few good friends, but that's about it. I haven't ever really had a boyfriend, and that's because I've built barriers around myself. Anyway, what actually happened to my mum?"

"We carried on desperately trying to help her but she still had a supplier, so I suppose we were fighting a lost cause. If you don't mind me saying that."

"Has she been cremated yet?"

"Yes, she was last week. We tried to find you but once you're over eighteen you go completely off our radar. We certainly didn't know that you were back in Fenningwood."

"I understand and thank you so much for coming over."

"You're welcome. Is your lunch date with someone special?"

"He is a special friend but as I said, I don't often let my guard down as I don't want to be hurt again."

"Maybe it's time, Jen. Maybe it's time."

"You could be so right, and thanks again for coming over."

"It's not a problem. Call me anytime."

*

In Lost Whistle, Danny, who usually dawdled and chatted during his delivery, had nearly completed his round and was trying to decide what he would say to Eddie. The words were forming in his mind, for he wanted to quell his anger and have a civil conversation. Something he had learned from a psychiatrist in prison as part of his rehabilitation. How he would feel when he saw Eddie would be anyone's guess. He dreaded telling Julie about that episode in his life and the subsequent flirtation with drug dealing. He wanted to leave it all behind him.

Sergeant Tomi Baker was still sitting on the bench on the village green, or triangle as it was sometimes called, wondering what to do with herself. Occasionally, someone would walk by and greet her but apart from that, she was alone. She was only in her early twenties and a bit of a rising star in the police, but she was in the south-east of England and came from Cumbria, or Westmorland as her grandparents preferred to call it, given their hometown's vicinity to the Lakes. But she was alone. She looked around at the trees that looked so tall and healthy, albeit the one on the green seemed to form a wide shelter. The countryside here was beautiful but her life felt pretty awful, especially with DI Hawley to answer to. She decided that she would book a few days off and go back home for a bit of unconditional love when there was a chance.

*

Jen was ready to meet Steve now and took the short walk to 'The Carrots'. Steve was already there and stood to greet her. She hugged him tightly and surprised him with a long, lingering kiss.

"This is my treat." Steve was speechless after that kiss, and before he could even reply, Jen was at the bar. "Can you open a tab for me, Greg? And I'll have a rosé, and we'll have Steve's usual, please." Greg smiled and nodded.

"So, how are you today, Jen, and this is a lovely surprise: thank you."

She proceeded to tell Steve about her walk to East Fenningwood and finding out that her mum had recently died. Then the visit from Janice. All of which was interspersed with tears. Janice had been so kind, not only now but twenty years ago as well. After their lunch, she suggested to Steve that they went back to her place as their conversation would be more private there.

"Do I need to bring anything?"

"No, I have everything we need. Come on, let's go."

They strolled off and Steve was taken by surprise when Jen put her hand in his. He was feeling a bit confused again.

Meanwhile, Dave was happily making his way home with his new laptop.

Danny wasn't at all confused like Steve; he was driving purposefully to Eddie's house in Fenningwood. His anger had yet to die down!

CHAPTER NINE

❉

In Lost Whistle, DI Hawley returned to find Tomi still sitting on the bench on the village triangle.

"Forensics now know that what killed Kath Megson was a poisonous powder called ricin. Who sent her the letter is completely unknown. They have one set of fingerprints, but chances are they're Danny's. How are you getting... Hang on, someone's going to Quilter's End. They both rushed over to the house. Hello! Are you looking for something particular?"

"I was just remembering a special lady who changed my life."

"And you are?"

"Why are you asking?"

"I'm Detective Inspector Hawley from Chrichton Police, and this is Sergeant Baker, and we're investigating Mrs Megson's murder." They both showed their photo ID.

"I'm Julie, and I was fostered by Aunt Kath for six years."

"Who were you fostered with?"

"Social Services – why?"

"Sorry, I meant to say, do you remember anyone who was fostered at the same time as you?"

"I only have one person that I have stayed in contact with."

"And her or his name?"

"Jen Greening. She lives in a place called Fenningwood."

"And what about any boys?"

Julie smiled and laughed. "We weren't allowed to mix with the boys."

"That's a bit hard to believe."

"Then don't believe it, if that's what you prefer. You didn't have to live it." Julie was now getting riled.

"You don't have to take that tone with me, and I didn't get your full name."

"Why would I want to tell someone who disbelieves me within a few minutes of talking to me what my name is? I will not be treated like that, so I'm off." Julie walked quickly across the green and into the Drunken Duck. They couldn't ask her questions with other people around.

"I don't understand what's wrong with these locals. I'm sure this is a conspiracy to hide the truth."

Tomi knew exactly what was wrong. "Perhaps we need to have a gentler approach with them, ma'am?"

"A gentler approach?" DI Hawley bellowed. "This is a murder investigation and one of them may well be the murderer."

"Or maybe none of them are."

She looked at Tomi and wondered, just for a moment, whether that could be a possibility.

*

Danny had arrived in Fenningwood but was a bit lost as he tried to find out where Eddie lived. He turned onto the High Street and passed a pub called 'The Bunch of Carrots'. Strange name, he thought, and then saw an estate agent called Snow and Co. They would know, he assured himself, and they certainly did. He was less than half a mile from his intended destination, so in a few minutes he was sitting outside Eddie's house, gathering his thoughts and trying to calm himself down. He would wait a couple of minutes before he knocked on the door.

Dave had also discovered Eddie by using his new laptop and was surprised to learn he had been in prison. Steve hadn't ever mentioned it, but then again, maybe he didn't know. What was also interesting was that Eddie had two known associates. A Danny Parker and a George Williams. He would have to do some more digging.

Steve and Jen were sitting on her sofa together with a chilled glass of rosé each. Jen had once again opened up to Steve and told him in more detail about the visit to East Fenningwood. Things that she wouldn't have told him in a public place. Her shock when she found out about her mum, watching the kids play, and her desire to give them some money.

"We would all like to do things like that, but where would we get the money from?"

"Steve, would you mind giving me a cuddle, please?" He smiled and took Jen in his arms, holding her tightly, though still affectionately. She turned to kiss him and once again it was a long, lingering kiss, then to Steve's surprise she grasped his right hand and placed it on her braless left breast. If he was confused before, he was now unnerved. He had wanted this moment for such a long time, but the reality of the situation befuddled him. Then Jen said something completely unexpected.

"Would you make love to me one day, please?"

He felt completely dumbfounded but mustered up an answer.

"Well, erm, okay, erm, if that's what you really want. It would certainly be with immense feeling from me." He knew that his words were clumsy. Jen put her left index finger on his lips.

"Let me talk. A lot has happened to me recently, and I've now started to let my guard down. Well, to you, anyway. And do you know why that is?"

Steve shook his head; he now had his right hand on Jen's right thigh as he felt awkward about where it was before.

"It's because I love you, Steve, and only these life lessons have made me realise. That's why I would like you to be the first man ever to make love to me, and hopefully the only man, if you understand what I'm saying."

Hearing her say it a second time didn't quash his unease. He viewed her as extremely emotionally vulnerable and didn't want her to feel that he had taken advantage of her in some way.

"What are you thinking, Steve? You seem deep in thought."

He hesitated. "I'm thinking about my feelings for you, as I have been in love with you for a good while now. Since I've got to know these latest facts about you, I think I love you even more."

"Thanks, Steve. Please stay with me for the afternoon."

He nodded his acceptance with tears gathering in his eyes.

*

Not far away, in Fenningwood, the atmosphere at Eddie's house was vastly different. Danny was at the door.

"What the hell do you want?"

"It's about the text message you sent me." Danny could feel his anger rising.

"I haven't sent you a text."

Danny had now intimidated Eddie, who shuffled backwards toward his kitchen.

"Yes, you did: 'It should have been him at Quilter's End'. That tells me you murdered Kath."

"It doesn't mean that at all."

"But you knew she had died, and I don't understand how."

"I have my contacts…"

Danny's temper boiled over and he hit Eddie, almost knocking him to the floor. Eddie reached for a long knife from the wooden block. Danny was enraged and kicked the knife from his hand. Eddie was shocked and when someone else appeared, he was wrestled to the ground with thumbs holding onto his throat until he fell silent. The murderer made a quick exit.

*

DI Hawley was trying to decide whether to find Julie in the Drunken Duck. Tomi suggested that they went back to Chrichton and researched who these people were, especially as she had just seen George Hicks arriving at the pub; she could do without another confrontation!

"Before we go back, let's see whether Rosemary is at home."

Her bicycle was there.

"Hello, Mrs Crumble."

"Do call me Rosemary, dear. I'm sorry, I don't think that I know your name, although I have seen you with that detective inspector."

"I'm Tomi. Sergeant Tomi Baker."

"It's lovely to meet you, and you have a delightful accent. Where are you from?"

"I'm from Cumbria, or Westmorland is the preference of some people…"

"Quite right, too. County names have been messed about with far too much, in my opinion. Where exactly in Westmorland?"

DI Hawley was becoming impatient with what she viewed as idle chit-chat. There was a job to get on with.

"Thank you for asking me, Rosemary. I'm actually from Appleby and—"

DI Hawley interrupted, but Rosemary and Tomi were bonding. "There's plenty of time for afternoon tea conversation another time. We have a murder to solve, and maybe it could be two."

"I wondered when you might pipe up, Chief Commander or whatever they call you."

"It is Detective Inspector, if you don't mind, and I'll get to the point. Who killed Kath Megson?"

"You're talking to me accusingly as if I would possibly know. Kath was a dear and lifelong friend and if I knew the answer to that question, I would have told the police at the very start. Your questioning technique is so abrasive that I don't want you in my house anymore, so please leave."

"I was only trying to—"

"Then don't. I know what I know and until you can learn to be civil, I'm not prepared to answer any questions. Good day."

Rachel and Tomi left without learning anything.

"I told you about these locals. They're definitely hiding something. I'd like to interview that postman, but I don't know where he lives."

"Would you like me to try and find out?"

"Tomi, I am a detective inspector and you are just a sergeant. If anyone can sniff him out, it will be me."

As they walked back to their car from Fipple Lane they could see George the journalist sitting outside the Drunken Duck with Julie. DI Hawley was incensed to see the two of them together, seemingly having a cosy chat and laughing.

"What is it with that man that he has to interfere?"

"Hello, Rachel," he called out, waving. Her blood felt as though it was boiling now.

"He's only doing his job and—"

"I don't care. He's a nuisance. Now get in the car and drive us back to Chrichton."

Tomi did as she was told and they drove back to Chrichton in silence.

*

Silence was far from what George was experiencing with Julie. She had reiterated everything about Quilter's End that he already knew, though it was obvious she knew nothing about Danny's past. He decided to explore whether she had unknowingly picked something up from him that George hadn't read about.

"Danny's a nice man, isn't he?"

"He seems to be. We've dated a few times but he's reluctant to talk about his past and I'm not sure why."

George knew exactly why but was hesitant to share Danny's former life, as he didn't feel it was his place.

"How did you meet Danny?"

"In here, funnily enough. I knew him as the postman, then we got chatting and thought maybe we have something in common. He's a chatty postman, though quiet when we go out. I need someone to warm to. Does that make sense?"

"It makes perfect sense, Julie. I can't even begin to imagine what it would feel like to go through what you've been through. Do you stay in touch with anyone from those days?"

"Just the one – Jen Greening. I was number 26 and Jen was number 28. We spent nearly six years together at Quilter's End. We're still in touch, though rarely see each other."

"Where does she live, if you don't mind me asking?"

"It's a place called Fenningwood. I haven't ever been there, but I'm going there at some point. We've both found Kath's death very emotional."

"What about Kath's husband?"

"I didn't really know him at all. He liked to be known as 'Sir' but he only dealt with the boys."

"Thanks, Julie. I need to get on my way but can I contact you in the future?" They exchanged phone numbers and George was off. The story was starting to come together.

*

Dave had wondered whether Eddie still lived there, and as he looked at everything about the man's social media profiles, Dave thought he recognised where Eddie lived. He decided to take a walk to see if he could find the place. A car sped past him.

Danny was racing back from Fenningwood, sweating profusely and still angry. He would need to shower when he got home, and he couldn't quite believe what had just happened.

Julie felt much more relaxed after her chat with George. DI Hawley had upset her. She was also wondering where Danny could be as it was very unusual for him to go out in the afternoon so early, though he would no doubt turn up with a story of some sort. She was starting to feel suspicious about him.

Before George left Lost Whistle, he took the opportunity to see Rosemary and retain her confidence. He enjoyed tea and cake with her, from bone china cups, of course, and then had a couple of questions.

"Rosemary. First of all, thank you, and I was wondering why your house is called 'The Witch's Wash'. Is it historical in some way?"

"The name dates back centuries, apparently, so let's go into the back garden. This huge pond with that rotting seat on a long arm are reputed to be the tool and water where witches were drowned. Maybe I should get it working again for that ghastly police inspector!" They both smiled. "Her sergeant is a complete delight, though."

"Thank you, Rosemary. I feel educated." He couldn't help noticing an open door to her garage that showed a car inside. Why didn't she drive it? A question for another day, he thought.

*

Dave was making his way to what he believed was Eddie's house, but wandered slowly as he didn't often walk along this road and had forgotten that the houses were a fair size. He wondered whether he would see Eddie. He recognised the car from images he had seen on the internet, and also noticed that the front door was open. What should he do? He decided to walk up the pathway and called out, "Hello?" but there wasn't an answer, so he took a long breath and went inside. Straight ahead, he could see a person lying on the floor of the kitchen, a large knife near his side, though no sign of any blood at all. He recognised the face as Eddie. What on earth should he do now?

CHAPTER TEN

❊

DI Hawley and Tomi Baker were back at Chrichton Police Station researching various people. All they found out was that Julie's surname was Miller, from the electoral roll, so they now knew her address, but there were no social media profiles at all. They didn't bother with Rosemary as they knew where she was, and if her bicycle was there, she was at home.

Tomi wondered whether this was wise but then a revelation about Danny took her attention. "I've found something, ma'am."

DI Hawley liked to be addressed in this way, despite having been Rach or Rachel when she was a constable.

"What is it?"

"Danny is Daniel John Parker, who has been in prison for car theft and arson. I wonder if Julie knows that. He has—"

"Right, get in the car, now. We have his address as well so we'll go there."

"I was going to say—"

"You can tell me some other time. Let's just get on our way."

*

Dave had called the police and they were there very quickly. He was standing outside Eddie's house wondering what was going to happen next. When the police arrived, he was sternly told to 'stay put,' although he didn't have any plans to go anywhere. They confirmed that Eddie was dead.

"So, what are *you* doing here?"

"I was just walking past, saw that the door was open and wanted to check that everything was okay."

"What is he to you?"

"Nothing, I was just walking up to the common and this is the easiest way to get there from where I live in Station Road."

A radio message came through to say that the deceased male was Edward Pitcher.

"Do you know him?"

Another message came through that he had a brother called Steven Pitcher.

"Do you know him?"

"It can't… Oh, hang on. I think that may be Steve. I don't ever use his surname, but he did once say that he had a brother that lived in Fenningwood somewhere. I've walked past this house so many times but never knew."

"Have you got Steven's phone number?"

Dave, although being a bit 'fingers and thumbs' because of what was happening, scrolled through his phone and found 'Steve.'

"Are you sure that is Steven Pitcher's phone number?"

"Yes. Yes, I'm sure."

The policeman phoned. The call woke Steve and Jen in her bed, despite it only being mid-afternoon.

"You need to answer it, Steve. It might be a new job."

"Hello. Steve, here."

"Is that Steven Pitcher?"

He felt suddenly very cold. Jen sensed that something was wrong.

"Yes it is. Who's asking, please?"

"I'm Constable Chris Austen from the local police; we believe that we have found your brother Edward, who has sadly passed away."

Jen was now rubbing his back to soothe him.

"Yes, Eddie is my brother. He lives in Common Road, though we rarely speak, and I think he rarely leaves the house."

"I'm really sorry to have to tell you this, but we need someone to identify his body."

"Sorry, I'm a bit in shock so…"

"That's completely understandable, sir."

"I'll be there in less than ten minutes."

"Thank you, sir, and can you bring some identification, please?"

"Yes, of course." He turned to Jen. "That was…"

She affectionately put her index finger on his lips. "I know. You had your phone on loudspeaker. Let's make ourselves look decent, then we can walk over there in a few minutes. Oh, and thank you. I love you even more now." Steve could feel tears welling in his eyes. What a mixture of emotions he was experiencing at this moment!

*

Dave was fretting. He was trusted to stand outside with a guarding officer rather than be locked in a police car. Then forensics arrived in a van. First of all, they got a full fingerprint from the doorbell that could be quickly analysed in their van, and another on the architrave of the kitchen.

DI Hawley and Tomi Baker were on their way back to Lost Whistle to see Danny, whilst George Hicks was planning his trip to Fenningwood the next day. Julie had gone from the Drunken Duck to Rosemary's house and they were having some tea and wondering what DI Hawley was trying to achieve. The chances of finding the killer in the village were minimal at best. When the police arrived, Danny wasn't at home.

"Let's go to Julie's now we know where she lives."

Again, no answer, despite Tomi being sent around the back to look. A wasted journey, so they headed back to Chrichton.

*

Steve and Jen's journey was unexpected. They left Jen's flat in Church Lane for the short walk to Common Road. They walked hand in hand, and Dave was very relieved to see them. Jen gave him a hug, quickly followed by Steve doing the same. Dave could smell the aroma of Jen on him; he was pleased for them. Steve announced himself to a police officer.

"Hello, I'm Steve Pitcher and I've arrived to identify the body of my brother," he announced, showing his driving licence.

"Thank you for getting here so promptly. Is Mrs Pitcher coming in as well?"

"She isn't Mrs Pitcher yet so she can stay with Dave."

Dave beamed at her, and she asked him a question. "Was that the most obscure marriage proposal that I have ever heard?"

"It certainly sounded like it to me." Dave put his arm around Jen, but then activity started up.

A member of the forensic team came out of their van and shouted, "Governor, we have two matches to one person, and we can see who he is. Would you like to see?"

"Yes, of course," he said and went into the converted van. He didn't close the side door and Jen could hear them talking about a Daniel John Parker who lives in a place called Lost Whistle, but there was trace of their compatriot, George Williams, who was the first culprit in some thoughts. They needed to question Daniel Parker in Lost Whistle. Jen was wondering whether she should phone Julie, and then Steve appeared.

"Gosh, what an experience." Steve had visibly paled. "He's certainly gone, and now I need to make funeral arrangements. I have no idea what to do, who to invite and how to I invite them; I can't think of any relatives that I have any contact with."

Jen hugged him tightly and kissed his cheek. "Don't worry. I'm back in the estate agents tomorrow; we can sort a lot out for you. Anyway, come on. You could do with a shower after this experience. Are you okay, Dave?"

"Yes, I'm just a bit shaken up. Shall we meet up in 'The Carrots' around 7-ish?"

"We'll see you there."

Steve and Jen went off to share her rather luxurious shower room.

The Fenningwood police were trying to work out the exact location of Lost Whistle. They needed to make contact and the nearest police station appeared to be Chrichton, according to a message sent by their station officer, so Constable Chris Austen prepared to phone them.

"How on earth do I say that, Sarge?"

"I thought you might ask, so I looked it up; it is pronounced: 'cryton.' How these names are dreamt up is anyone's guess. Anyway, here's the CID number."

"Thanks, Sarge. I'll call them."

Sergeant Tomi Baker picked up the phone and was chatting away, noting down the salient information, then started to ask further questions about the area of Fenningwood.

"I've told you before that this isn't a place for idle chit-chat. Who are you talking to?"

"Excuse me, Chris: DI Hawley, this is not 'idle chit-chat', as you call it. I am getting a serious lead about Danny's activities."

With that, DI Hawley snatched the phone from Tomi's hand and bellowed into the phone, "Who the hell are you?"

Chris was taken aback, then calmed himself. "I'm Chris from Fenningwood Police. May I ask who you are, please?"

Rachel stood up. "I, am Detective Inspector Hawley, and I, am in charge."

"I'm very pleased for you, ma'am, but can you hand me back to Tomi, please? We were part way through me asking for help regarding a murder."

"I, am in charge, you know."

Chris sighed and said to Tomi. "What a ghastly woman!"

"Don't get me started. So, how can we help?"

"Are you familiar with a place called Lost Whistle?"

"Familiar, Chris!" She chuckled. "I've been there twice today as we had a murder there a couple of days ago. What's your interest?"

"We have a very recent murder here, by that I mean within the last hour or so, and some new fingerprints match those of someone who was released from prison about ten years ago, and lives in Lost

Whistle. His name is Daniel John Parker: any thoughts?"

"I certainly have. That's Danny the postman. We tried to see him a short while ago but he wasn't in, how far is – did you say Fenningwood?" Chris confirmed that Tomi had it right. "How far is Lost Whistle from Fenningwood?"

"It's about fifty minutes, so if he has gone straight home he should be there by now. I know we're talking about murders but it sounds like a lovely place."

"It is. There are funny street names, and a pub called the Drunken Duck, not that I've ever been in there. I'm happy to live alone, though I don't like going out alone."

"Maybe if I end up coming there, we could pop in?"

Tomi let her hair down and then put it back into a ponytail.

"Maybe, yeah. In the meantime, we need to get over to Danny's and then I'll call your mobile. Thanks for the lead, Chris."

"Finished your chit-chat, then?"

Tomi chose to ignore her comment.

"We need to get over to Lost Whistle and now. I'll explain on the way and please, just for once, trust me."

Rachel reluctantly got into the car.

*

In Fenningwood, Dave was at a bit of a loose end. The police had released him, the source of his recent searching was dead, and he already knew about Danny. What next? Maybe it was time to find out about this George Williams, although Dave was a bit wary as he knew that there had been drugs involved. It made him feel uneasy, though no less inquisitive.

After their shower, Steve and Jen went to meet Dave. They also ordered a bite to eat.

"What a day, Steve. How are you feeling?"

"I feel a bit confused, if I'm honest, Dave. Having not seen Eddie for years, it was odd to see him just lying on the floor as if no years had passed. I'm shocked that he was murdered, though I have no idea of the company he kept. I'm sure the police will tell me."

"I'm sure they will, too," Dave said knowingly.

When Dave went to the bar, Jen asked Steve if he would stay with her tonight. Of course he would, and in bed that night, Jen asked him a question.

"When the police asked if Mrs Pitcher was going to help identify Eddie's body, you said, 'She isn't Mrs Pitcher yet,' and I wondered what you meant."

"It was a very clumsy way of asking you whether you will marry me: will you?"

"Yes! Yes! Yes! Stevie Pitcher, I love you!"

Once again, Steve had tears in his eyes.

"The last person to call me Stevie was my mum and she died about ten years ago now. She would also call me Ste in her own Scottish way. We'll need to go ring shopping."

"There's no need." Jen popped to the kitchen and returned with some string and a pair of scissors. She tied a bit around the third finger of her left hand and said to Steve, "Cut the string and tie a knot." Steve did exactly that. "That's the knot that makes us one. It's a promise never to be broken. Discreet wedding rings can come when we have a date and location sorted out. Is that okay?" Steve nodded and kissed her, then they snuggled up for a good night's sleep.

*

In Lost Whistle, Tomi and Rachel arrived at Danny's.

"The bonnet is still hot," Tomi mentioned, though there was no reaction from DI Hawley. She then knocked on Danny's door. He appeared and was wet, wearing only a towel. "You've been out all afternoon, Danny. Where did you go?"

"I just went to see a mate. Anyway, what's that to you?"

"I just wondered where you had been."

"To be honest, it's none of your business."

"But what if it is my business? Your fingerprints have been found on a doorbell and kitchen door frame in a place called Fenningwood, where we have found a recent murder victim. That makes it my business." Danny shuffled awkwardly. "Where were you this afternoon between midday and 16:00?"

"No comment."

That was all Tomi needed to hear. She read him the standard charge and told him to get dressed. DI Hawley guarded the front door and Tomi the back.

The inspector drove back to Chrichton with Tomi and the handcuffed Danny on the back seat. Tomi would phone Chris Austen in Fenningwood and let him know. He would be in Chrichton first thing tomorrow. Working together had worked out well.

CHAPTER ELEVEN

❖

Jen woke up around 6:00am and looked at Steve beside her, and then at the knotted string on her finger. She leaned over and kissed his back; he gave a mild sigh.

Danny's night had been altogether different in Chrichton Police Station: a hard bed, no-one to talk to, and a day full of regrets to dwell on. How would he get out of this situation? He needed help.

In Lost Whistle, Julie was woken by a message arriving on her phone at 6:30am: 'DID YOU MAKE DANNY DO IT?' She cried and, in her panic, hid her phone under her pillow. Maybe she had dreamt it, so maybe it would go away, but she knew it wouldn't. What should she do? She needed to phone the police but was it too early to call Tomi Baker's mobile? She certainly didn't want to talk to DI Hawley. She went downstairs to put the kettle on and decide over a cup of tea; then she would phone Tomi. At 6:32am, Jen received a message on her phone: 'WERE YOU DRIVING THE CAR THAT KILLED ROBERT?' She looked at it in disbelief.

The sound had woken Steve.

"Jen, what's wrong?"

"I've just had this awful message." She showed it to him.

"We have to tell the police now."

"But you have to go to work."

"I know, and I will once I know they're on their way. Let me find that name and phone number." He was still half asleep and bursting for a wee, so he got that out of the way and then splashed his face with the water he was washing his hands with.

"Ah, here we are, Chris Austen; I'll phone him now."

Jen was pacing up and down, and Steve's phone was on

loudspeaker.

"Hi, Chris, this is Steve Pitcher, Eddie's brother from yesterday. My girlfriend Jen, the future Mrs Pitcher, has received a nasty message from someone saying: 'were you driving the car that killed Robert?' It's a Lost Whistle reference and we don't know what to do. Can you help at all, please?"

"A detective from there briefed me about all the things that have been happening, and I'm actually just on my way to interview a suspect in the murder of your brother, and his girlfriend has received a nasty message as well."

"Is that Julie?" Jen called out.

"It would be wrong of me to say, but do you know her?"

"She was number 26 and I was number 28."

"You've lost me, I'm afraid. Can I call you when I'm on my way back from Lost Whistle? I would also like to see you today, if that's possible."

They both said they were happy with that. Chris briefed his station sergeant, who said he would update Detective Chief Inspector (DCI) Emily Harris. Chris finally found Chrichton Police Station.

Tomi had phoned Julie and promised to go and see her once the interview was over. When Chris Austen arrived, he and Tomi hit it off completely: they clearly had a common cause, which was justice, and got themselves prepared to interview Danny. DI Hawley left them to it as she thought they were 'barking up the wrong tree,' as the raccoon hunters would say.

Danny chose not to have legal representation and answered every open question identically: Where were you…? How do you know…? Why did you…? With the same words: "No comment." As they had fingerprint evidence, they asked the local magistrate that he be remanded in custody for fourteen days. Permission was granted and this gave them time to build up their case.

*

In Fenningwood, Jen was back at work in Snow and Co. after an extraordinary couple of days and catching up with her work issues. The text message was still very prominent in her mind when another incident brought her even more turmoil. George Hicks had arrived in Fenningwood but didn't know how to find Eddie's house, though he felt sure someone would know Eddie. He parked in Carrot's Crescent, which ran from the High Street to South Road. It had the Bunch of Carrots pub on one corner, and Snow and Co. on the other corner. The pub was closed so he went into Snow and Co.

"Hello. Can I help you?"

"I hope so. My name is George Hicks from the *Chrichton and District Examiner*, and I'm trying to find a couple of people: Jen Greening, and Eddie Pitcher. Would you know them at all?" Jen just stared at him. "May I sit down, please?" She nodded her approval. "Are you okay?"

"Yes… Yes… I'm Jen Greening and Eddie Pitcher is, or was, my boyfriend's brother."

George could tell that it was time to be gentle.

"Thank you, Jen. Part way through you changed Eddie from 'is' to 'was.' What made you do that?"

"Eddie was murdered yesterday and I think the police know who did it. I also think that he, the murderer, is in Chrichton Police Station at the moment."

George's mind was working overtime.

"Can I…?" Steve rushed in.

"Jen, I have Chris Austen from the police on the phone. Can we go somewhere private? Apologies, client, she'll be right back."

Chris explained to Jen that Julie had also received a text from the same number, which they were having trouble tracing. Probably because it was pay-as-you-go and wasn't registered to anyone, not that this would stop them trying.

"Julie's text said, 'DID YOU MAKE DANNY DO IT?' Oh, and Jen, I now understand your reference to 26 and 28. Can I come over this afternoon, please? I'm aware that you need to get back to your client."

"Actually, he's a journalist from Chrichton."

"How very interesting. Can you hold on to him for 20 minutes and I'll come straight there? I'll also have Tomi Baker from Chrichton Police with me, who's investigating the Lost Whistle cases. Is that okay?"

"Yes, Chris, that will be fine. It should be easy enough without really telling him anything that isn't already known. See you very shortly."

"Are you sure that you'll be okay, Jen?"

"There's nothing to worry about, Steve. I'll see if the boss will let me use a meeting room, otherwise we can go to our flat. I'll call you if I need you, now get back to work, you daft wotsit, though don't forget that I love you."

Steve smiled and went back to work.

"Hello, George. Sorry about that but I had to take a call from the police. Now, where were we?"

"That's not a problem. What did they need to know?"

"They were just updating me on a couple of bits."

"And they have someone in custody, you say?"

"If those are the words for it, though to be honest I don't know the details and wouldn't expect them to tell me. Anyway, you came here to ask me about Eddie, so how can I help you?"

"You say that he was the brother of your boyfriend and…"

"Are you implying that I'm lying by doubting that he was my boyfriend's brother?"

"No, no, not at all, and I'm really sorry, I worded that question in a very clumsy way. What I wanted to ask was whether I could see Eddie's house."

"I'll deal with the quick bit. Common Road, where Eddie lived, is sealed off by the police with only residents and relatives allowed, so you won't be able to go there. Yes, he was the brother of my boyfriend Steve, although they rarely, if ever, spoke to or saw each other. Oddly enough, I found out just the other day that he was fostered for a while at Quilter's End as well, but the boys and girls weren't allowed to mix, though Steve told me that he was number 27, if that means anything to you."

"Luckily it does, Jen, as Julie explained it all to me; and I do understand that you weren't allowed to mix with the boys."

"So, what do you want to know about me? You seem to know so much already."

"I was…"

The door opened with a uniformed policeman and a young woman, smartly dressed, though casual by comparison.

"Hello, Jen. Chris Austen, the policeman from yesterday and…"

"Well, well, well: Tomi Baker, how lovely to see you."

Jen looked at George strangely as he obviously knew the person with Chris.

"Sorry, but I'm confused, Chris. Who exactly is who? I know who you are, by the way."

"This is Sergeant Tomi Baker from Chrichton CID. Your go, Tomi."

"He is George Hicks from the local newspaper in Chrichton."

"I must apologise, Tomi. When Chris said your name I was expecting a male."

"Don't worry, Jen. You aren't the first and you certainly won't be the last. Anyway, we're here now."

Jen's boss ushered them into a private room and took orders for teas and coffees. Chris started.

"Are you okay with a journalist in the room, Jen?"

"No I'm not, really. I don't mean any offence, George, but can you wait somewhere else, please? The 'Carrots' serves a nice lunch, and then I'll come and find you."

George understood and politely left the room. Tomi had noticed the knotted string on Jen's finger.

"Are you and your boyfriend getting married?"

"Yes, we're hoping to soon, with our friend Dave as a witness, and I'm hoping that Julie could come along as a witness as well. What makes you ask?"

"You have a beautifully knotted ring that says so much, but you're going to be a very wealthy young woman soon: wouldn't you prefer something more valuable?"

"I think I understand where you are coming from, but you need to understand me a bit more. As an aside, Steve doesn't know anything about the money yet, so please don't tell him. I'm a kid from East Fenningwood, a mile or so up the road: a social housing estate hidden behind trees with its own shop. I'm mixed race, have no idea who my dad is, and my mum is a dead drug addict who left me wandering the streets when I was twelve years old. I was rescued by a social worker called Janice, and then Aunt Kath in Lost Whistle, so you see: I haven't ever known what it's like to have money. Do I want a flashy ring? No, I just want the man that I love. Do I want a flashy car? I haven't ever owned a car yet, so it would be a waste of money. What I would like to do is to spend money on a new playground in East Fenningwood. I'll probably buy an unobtrusive house to live in. Apart from that, it's just a few numbers. Do you understand me?"

Chris and Tomi looked at Jen in stunned silence.

"Jen, I can only applaud your humility and honesty, but I have to ask you: do you know Daniel John Parker?"

"Is that Danny the postman?"

"Yes it is."

"I only know him by name as Julie has had a couple of dates with him. Other than that: no, nothing."

"Jen, would you object to having a DNA test?"

"I have no objection, although I do wonder why you ask."

"Eddie and Danny had a third person within their circle that seemed to influence them, and he is of Caribbean origin; I wondered if it might give a clue. No racism intended, of course."

"You aren't being racist at all, Chris. If it helps to understand everything a bit more, then let's do it. I have nothing to hide so what do I need to do?"

"You'll have to come to the police station but so you don't look like a criminal, you can sit in the front seat."

"I remember my first ride in a police car when I was twelve years old. So much has changed in twenty years."

"Tomi, I need to know more about what's gone on in Lost Whistle. Can I come over tomorrow? Maybe we could have dinner at the Drunken Duck?"

Jen chuckled at the memory of a place that she hadn't ever entered, though knew so well. Tomi tingled.

"Feel free to stay over, Chris." Then Tomi left to return to Chrichton.

While Jen was having her DNA test, Chris was called to DCI Emily Harris' office.

"I think we should have a meeting or video call with these people from Lost Whistle and Chrichton. What do you think, Detective Sergeant Austen?"

Chris was momentarily confused and looked at Emily blankly.

"I'm asking for your opinion, Sergeant."

"I'm confused as I'm not…"

"Yes, you are, and congratulations, Chris – it's well deserved."

"Well erm… Thank you, ma'am, I…"

"Don't thank me, Chris. You're the well-deserving person we need as part of our team, and you can celebrate later. So, what do you think about us all getting together?"

"I think it's something we need to do as a matter of urgency, and I believe that we need to do it in person as I would like you to look their DI in the eye."

"Okay. Can you organise that for tomorrow and give me a full briefing in a couple of hours, please?"

"Will do." Chris then went to find Jen, as he had promised to drop her back in Fenningwood. "We'll probably have your results in about three days."

"Wow, that's quick."

"Yes, and we're having a case conference tomorrow, so I may need another chat."

"Just give me a call and I can get Steve as well if you need him."

Jen popped into the 'Carrots' to tell George that she needed to get back to work, though if he arranged a day and time, rather than turning up by chance, she could probably find him a space. She was getting a little suspicious of him!

"I understand, Jen, though what about your boyfriend Steve? What's he up to?"

"He'll be working somewhere. Why do you need to know?"

"No particular reason. I'll just take a wander around and give you a call at some point."

Jen rushed back to Snow and Co. and apologised to her boss, who was completely understanding.

"With all that you have gone through, Jen, and with all you have had to deal with, I'm grateful that you take such a small amount of time off."

"Thanks, Maddie. It's a bit of a strain sometimes, but everyone is so supportive."

"Congratulations on getting engaged. I've always wondered whether you and Steve would become a couple at some point, and I'm delighted for you."

"Thank you, though now it's time that I got some work done."

*

Chris phoned Tomi as he thought she would be back in Chrichton by now, and she was.

"You don't give a girl a chance to catch her breath, do you, Chris?"

"It's Sergeant Chris, now."

"Are you saying you've been promoted?"

"I certainly have, and—"

"Congratulations! Congratulations! I'm so pleased for you."

"Why, thank you, Sergeant Baker." They both laughed. "I need to rearrange tomorrow as my DCI would like you and your boss to come here for a case conference. Is 10 o'clock okay?"

"Hang on, I'll check."

Chris could hear faint talking and a raised voice in the background.

"We'll be there, Chris. See you tomorrow."

Chris was now wondering what to wear the next day, as he had only ever worn uniform before.

Jen decided she would phone Julie that evening to ask whether she would be a witness to her and Steve getting married.

For George Hicks, there suddenly seemed to be another opportunity as he walked along Station Road and came across a van with the slogan, 'Steve Pitcher: cleaner of offices, windows and shops'. There wasn't any sign of him, though George was concerned that he had only had a fleeting glance of him at Snow and Co. He wasn't in a hurry and so decided to wait. Dave could see George and his notebook hanging around Steve's van from his vantage point in his room opposite. It made him feel uneasy, so he decided to go out and discover what was going on.

"Good afternoon," he called out as he closed the red door behind him.

"Good afternoon to you, too. Can you spare me a few minutes, please?"

"As long as you aren't undertaking a survey, then maybe I can."

"I'm George Hicks, a journalist from the *Chrichton and District Examiner*. I'm trying to understand a bit more about recent murders. Do you know anything about them?"

"I know that there was a murder in Common Road, though I'm not aware of any others."

"Can I ask for your name, please?"

"You can, but you're making me very wary so..."

"Hello, Dave. Everything okay?" Steve called out.

"So, Dave it is then."

QUILTER'S END

Steve looked at George, feeling some disdain towards him.

"Were you the bloke sitting with Jen at Snow and Co. earlier?"

"Yes, I was, so you must be Steve."

"I am, but what is it to you and who are you anyway?"

"I'm George Hicks, a journalist from Chrichton, and I've been investigating the Lost Whistle…"

"And then you thought you would try and dig up some dirt about my brother Eddie? Well, think again. You'll get nothing from me or Dave and Jen didn't know him, so the best thing you can do is disappear back to where you came from. What about you, Dave?"

"I'm with you totally, Steve, so George, you would do yourself a favour by leaving now."

"Are you threatening me, Dave?"

"Not at all. I'm making an emotional plea to treat people with respect and thoughtfulness and leave them alone when they're grieving."

"But—"

"No buts. You leave this town now, as we are just about to do."

Steve and Dave got into the van and just drove.

"Where am I going, Dave?"

"Why not go to the Old Mill and ask about weddings? That will give Jen a surprise."

George was walking back towards Carrots Crescent and saw Jen without a client.

"Hello again."

"I thought you were on your way back to Chrichton."

"I am but…"

"Never mind 'I am but'. You've upset Steve so please leave now."

George got to the door and said, "Can I just—"

Jen stood up. "No, you can't. Now please leave before I call the police."

George knew when he had gone too far and started to walk away.

He would see what he could find out from Julie tomorrow.

Jen phoned Julie, who was delighted to hear the news and agreed to be a witness.

"Please come over for lunch tomorrow, Ju."

Julie hadn't been called by that shortened name for over fourteen years now, and it was when she went chasing after a ball they were playing with on the green in Lost Whistle and Jen yelled for her to avoid a car being driven erratically.

"Of course I will."

"I'll meet you at the station about 12:30pm."

Jen waited for Steve to get back home and gave him a front door key that she'd had cut at the convenience store. She was delighted that he had been to the Old Mill, and Steve was looking forward to meeting Julie. They snuggled up and reflected on the day.

"Maybe we'll be out of the woods soon."

"I'll never be out of the woods, Steve, that's where I was born, and those people need to be cared for."

CHAPTER TWELVE

❊

Julie woke up excited for her day out, though had to get the bus to Chrichton quite early as the following one would make her late. Also, there wasn't a direct train to Fenningwood so there was that change to consider as well. A shower, a few bits in a bag, then a short while later she was on the bus and on her way. Jen sounded like the quiet, though strong-willed person she had always been. Julie couldn't wait to see her.

Tomi and DI Hawley arrived at Fenningwood Police Station, quite a way out on the north side of the town towards the motorway. Much to DI Hawley's horror, Tomi greeted Sergeant Austen with a kiss on the cheek and a congratulatory card.

"Well done, Chris."

"Thank you. That's so kind."

"Is this appropriate? This is a place of work."

They both looked at Rachel almost pitifully, and Chris took them to the meeting room to meet DCI Emily Harris.

"Thank you both so much for coming here. What I would like to understand is what has happened so far, so that we know exactly where we are now. I would also like us to use our chosen given names rather than anything hierarchical; and that means I am Emily, and he is Chris, and you are Tomi and Rachel. Just as an aside, what is Tomi short for?"

"Thomasina. I think my dad just got bored with saying such a long name."

"What a great answer, Tomi. Let's summarise where we are: Firstly, Kath Megson was killed using an envelope containing powdered poison..."

"Not necessarily the first murder, Emily."

"Go on, Tomi."

"Kath's husband Robert was killed in a car accident, although there are unsubstantiated views that he may have been killed deliberately as he was so disliked around the village, as well as by the previously fostered boys."

"That is very useful, Tomi, and thank you. Let's chalk him up as being the first possible victim, but who are the possible suspects?"

Tomi spoke again. "Eddie Pitcher is the obvious one, as in a text very shortly after Kath had been murdered he wrote, 'It should have been him.' On the face of it, that says it should have been Kath's husband, but he had already been dead for five months, and Eddie surely would have known that, so who was 'him'? Was it indeed Robert? Was it Danny? Though if so, why send Danny the text, unless to make a false trail, or was it someone different completely?"

"You didn't ever share those thoughts with me."

"To be honest, Rachel, they only came into my thoughts a few minutes ago."

"That is really useful, Tomi, and we mustn't always go for the obvious. Chris, you mentioned a third person who was a mate of Eddie and Danny in prison."

"It's George Williams, a man seemingly of Caribbean origin who had a sentence for selling drugs, though from his records not the 'main man' at all, and that still remains a mystery. Coincidentally, he is known to have spent a lot of time around Fenningwood thirty or so years ago."

"Do we know where he is now?"

"No, we don't, although Jen Greening agreed to have a DNA test as she is the only part-Caribbean person that I can think of around here."

"Well done, Chris, and keep the confidence of the family. It is so important that they trust us."

*

In Lost Whistle, George had arrived at Julie's, having decided he may be able to glean some information from her. He parked (as usual) in the Drunken Duck car park, and then saw Rosemary cycling by.

"Hello, Rosemary."

"George! How delightful to see you."

"I'm off to see Julie, and then would it be okay to pop by afterwards, please?"

"That would be delightful, George. I'm so worried about all the goings on around here."

George smiled, thinking that he must get a closer look at Rosemary's garage. He then headed off to Wind Way where Julie lived. There wasn't an answer and he wondered whether to wait.

After the blow that knocked him to the ground, he was stunned and then felt the thumbs on his windpipe.

Jen and Steve had talked about the 'Old Mill' where they hoped to get married and she suggested that they go there for lunch with Julie, and invite Dave as well.

"It's a bit pricey there, Jen."

"I know, but I haven't seen Julie for fourteen years and it'll be nice for us all to be together, although we'll need to find a registrar as well once we've set a date.

"You're right, Jen. We only live the one time, and I'm so lucky to be blessed with you. I'll make sure that I'm home by midday. Oh, I love you, by the way." Jen blew him a kiss before he drove away.

Dave had finished his short early shift by 11:30am so there was time before he got to Jen's flat. Jen had booked a taxi for the four of them and was excited at the prospect of seeing Julie.

In Lost Whistle, it was pandemonium. The replacement postman for Danny had found a dead body in Julie's very small front garden behind a hedge. The uniformed police were there, though without the authority to move the body, and then Detective Constable Billy Wallis arrived, trying to think of what Tomi would do. He called forensics and they would be on their way; he asked the uniformed officers to stay on guard; he phoned Tomi but there was no answer, so he tried a text saying that there was a new murder.

"My goodness," she blurted out. "There's been another murder in Lost Whistle."

"You had both better get back there now, and Chris, you go and help too. Use blues if you need to."

Julie was on her way too, albeit in the opposite direction from Lost Whistle to Fenningwood. Jen was not supposed to be finishing for a couple of hours, although she had in fact booked the whole day off. Dave was showered and ready very early, and Steve was clambering down his ladder to put away his window-cleaning equipment. He was still a bit concerned about money, although cancelling his flat rental would save him a significant amount. He assumed that Jen was pretty much okay financially as he'd known her a fair few years now; she wasn't ever extravagant, he hadn't ever known her go on holiday, and she earned a decent salary. She had his respect as well as his love.

In Lost Whistle, Tomi, Rachel and Chris had arrived.

"What's going on then?" DI Hawley barked at her detective constable.

"Well done, Billy," Tomi said on her way past. Forensics were there, although with little to report other than asphyxiation. Tomi and Rachel looked and knew that it was George Hicks.

"We'll need some more formal identification so find some family, Billy."

"Please wouldn't have gone amiss."

"What is it with you, Baker?" Chris raised his eyebrows, and Tomi winked and turned to the postman.

"Hello, I'm Sergeant Baker from Chrichton CID, and I'm sorry that we've kept you hanging around. How are you feeling?"

"I'm a bit shocked as I'm only covering this while Danny is away somewhere. I certainly didn't expect anything like this to happen."

"Did you know the victim?"

"No I didn't, but if he lived around here I probably wouldn't anyway, as I tend to deliver in Chrichton town centre."

"You've given a statement to Billy so I'll let you on your way and hope that the rest of your day is less eventful."

DI Hawley reappeared. "I'm going back to the station. I'm sure that your new friend will give you a lift!" And with that, she was gone. Tomi and Chris looked at each other in relief.

"We'd better move your car, actually, Chris, as I think a bus comes up here and it won't get through at the moment. We can park at the Drunken Duck."

George's car was also in the car park, and they would have to deal with that, then as they walked back to Julie's house, Rosemary appeared on her bicycle.

"Oh, Tomi: thank goodness I've seen you. Is it true that there has been another murder?"

"I'm afraid so, Rosemary. It happened in Julie's front garden."

"Oh, poor Julie. Is she okay?"

"I don't know as no-one can get hold of her at the moment."

"This is truly awful. Do we know who it was?"

"We do, Rosemary, but he hasn't been formally identified yet so it would be wrong of me to tell you, but it's George, the journalist."

"George? My goodness, and such a lovely man. Will you excuse me for interfering, but is this your young man?"

Tomi smiled a beaming smile.

"I should be so lucky, Rosemary. This is Sergeant Chris Austen from Fenningwood Police and we're working together on these cases."

"Well if—"

Tomi's phone rang. It was DI Hawley. Rosemary got on her way.

"Tomi, I'm afraid I must go away for a while. My mother has been taken very ill in the west country and I have to get down there straight away. Will you be okay?"

"I'll be okay, thank you, and Chris will let Emily Harris know. I think we'll probably release Danny, though, as our evidence now looks very thin."

"I agree, Tomi, just send me an update every few days and I'll let you know what I'm likely to be up to so everyone is up to date."

"You get off and support your mum and I'll see you soon. Chris, let's check Julie's garden in case there's any evidence, then I need to get back to Chrichton and I'll call you a bit later with an update."

"Okay, and one day we'll get around to that dinner date."

Tomi tingled again.

George's body was being taken away and despite a good look around, there was nothing to be found in Julie's garden. When they got back to the car park of the Drunken Duck, something had changed: George's car had gone from the car park! Instinctively, they both ran to see where it could have gone, but it had completely vanished! How could this happen with two detectives about 100m away? Was it a strangely coincidental car theft? Or was it George's killer who had stolen his life, his keys, and now his car?

"That will be left somewhere so we need some publicity. Do we have the registration number?"

"No, but we can easily get it. Will you come back to Chrichton to help me sort this out, please?"

"Of course, Tomi. Let's go."

*

Julie had enjoyed her journey as she hadn't been out, apart from to the shops, for such a long time. The bus ride to Chrichton was as usual on her shopping days, then there was the train ride to Scanning Junction. It reminded her how much beautiful countryside there was on the way. At Scanning it was easy to change onto a city train to Fenningwood, and she was very excited about seeing Jen after fourteen years.

Jen was equally excited, and everything was going well with Steve home and in the shower, and Dave had called to say that he was on the way over. Jen walked up to the station; Julie was getting up from her seat as the train slowed down; they were both feeling the same anticipation. Julie checked her phone was still on silent, although what happened next was far from silent. As Julie swiped her ticket to get her through the barrier, both she and Jen had big tears in their eyes. Initially it was a mild scream, and then a humming noise between them, like the two long-lost souls that they once were, and in a way had become to each other – in many ways, to themselves. It was time to build their friendship again as they walked down Station Road hand in hand. The smiles were unlikely to disappear from their faces.

Steve was delighted to meet Julie and embraced her in a way that she hadn't really experienced for some time. Yes, Danny had hugged her, though not in this warm way, but in reality, he was aiming for some kind of sexual gratification that she wasn't prepared to give. She could understand why Jen loved Steve. Dave was a little colder, largely because he was such a shy person, although mainly because he felt an immense amount of internal guilt that was unknown to anyone else, about having found his way into Jen's email account and knowing of the exchanges with Julie. Now wasn't the time for that, though: this was a celebration! The four of them clambered into the taxi that Jen had arranged and headed to the Old Mill for lunch. Next time, they hoped it would be for the wedding of Jen and Steve.

*

In Chrichton, Tomi and Chris had managed to arrange publicity, with a photo and the registration plate of George's car. It was published widely on social media, and on train bulletins. They were shocked by the rapid response. A train driver who had seen the post on social media spotted the car at the parking area for Chrichton North Station. He had also seen a person getting out of the driver's side. Tomi and Chris went to meet him at Chrichton Station. The train driver had a photo and it was clearly George's car; the man getting out had a long coat, a large hat, and kept his head down – the cameras confirmed this.

Chris looked at Tomi. "What on earth is going on here?"

Jen knew exactly what was going on, as although she had given the impression that she would just be available for lunch, having actually had the whole day to herself she had taken the train to Bunhill for an appointment at the registry office. In her handbag, which she was proud to have bought from the charity shop on the

High Street, she had confirmation of the date for her wedding to Steve, although it needed his signature to be confirmed absolutely. They were welcomed at the Old Mill.

"You must be Mr and Mrs Pitcher."

"Not quite," Steve said, looking in a puzzled way at Jen.

"I'll tell you at the table."

They were seated and four flute glasses and champagne arrived at the table, with an impeccably dressed waiter who popped the cork and slowly and gently poured. No overflowing and maximum bubbles. Jen proposed a toast:

"To special people, and to my beloved Steve, who I shall marry here one month from today, if he agrees."

Steve looked at Jen in amazement. "Have you really…?"

"Yes, I have really. Is that okay?"

"Okay? It's wonderful! Thank you so much." Quiet applause from waiting staff and others helped to make it a really fun atmosphere. Then something took Jen by surprise.

"I suppose that with your wedding coming up, you have plans for your inheritance. I have no idea what to do with mine."

For a second time Steve looked at Jen with amazement in his eyes. "What inheritance is this then?" he asked in a gentle rather than pointed way.

"Steve…" Jen briefly buried her head in her hands, and then swept her hair back and put it into another band to tidy it. "…Steve, firstly I'm sorry for keeping this from you, but something was important to me. I needed to know that it was me you wanted and loved, and I know that is the case. It's nothing to do with the money and… Oh, I'm so sorry as it sounds like I doubted you. I didn't really, and I'm so looking forward to becoming Mrs Pitcher and—"

"Jen, you're rambling now," Steve said, struggling to contain a giggle. "I know all of that and I love you. It really makes no difference."

"Thank you." Jen stood over him and hugged him for all she was worth.

"What is this inheritance anyway, Julie?"

"It's the house that is 'Quilter's End' where we lived for six years..."

"And where my brother Eddie stayed too!"

"So I hear, though it's now to be sold and Jen and I will be the only beneficiaries."

"I don't know anything about Lost Whistle apart from Eddie mentioning it a few times, then obviously Jen has enlightened me about it. Is Quilter's End a big house?"

"It is a very large house. It has eight bedrooms and three living rooms. To be honest I can't remember how many bathrooms or toilets, but it is worth a fair bit."

"When you say, 'a fair bit,' what exactly do you mean?"

"You'd best refill your glass, Steve. It'll be in excess of £2.5 million." The table fell silent, and the waiter preparing to take food orders retreated discreetly.

"That's why I know I can help the people of East Fenningwood, Steve."

"You really are the most big-hearted person that I have ever known, and gosh, I shall be so proud to be your husband."

The whole afternoon was glorious and they returned to Jen and Steve's afterwards. Julie stayed the night, oblivious to the fact that there had been a murder in her front garden!

*

In Chrichton, the mystery of George's car had been partly resolved in that it had been spotted in the car park of Chrichton North Station by a train driver, but who had driven it there, and what happened to them after that remained unknown. It was making Tomi and Chris anxious and they were concerned about the safety of Jen and Julie. Danger seemed to be closing in!

CHAPTER THIRTEEN

❖

After Chris had gone back to Fenningwood, Tomi felt very alone. Forensics were dealing with George's car at Chrichton North Station car park, and then it would be towed away to a safe place. She was, however, still perturbed that someone unknown still had a key. Also, what other keys did they have? Was George's house safe? For a moment it all felt a bit much, but then Billy arrived with his seemingly permanent delighted demeanour.

"Sorry, Billy. It's late and you should be going home. I really haven't spent much time with you today."

"Don't worry, Tomi. You look as if you need a bit of a rest, but I'm in a bit of a quandary."

"That's intriguing. What's up?"

"I've been trying to find relatives of George Hicks, but the only people I can find are Rachel Hawley and her mother in the west country, who is clearly his sister. I kept thinking that I must have made a mistake, but time and again I'm getting the same answer and I'm really worried."

"Don't be worried, Billy. Facts are facts, we then have to deal with them."

Tomi's phone rang. It was Chris, telling her that Superintendent Pete Meachant wanted to see them all in the morning.

"I think you could have hit the nail on the head, Billy. Meet me here at 6:30am tomorrow. Oh, and best be 'togged up', please, as we'll be going to Fenningwood. Well done, mate." He felt quietly proud.

*

Jen had just boiled the kettle when Julie appeared from the spare room. They hugged again like long-lost sisters, although they were both a bit bleary-eyed from an afternoon of celebration.

"Can I visit Quilter's End one last time before it's sold, please? I would just like to have a look around after all these years."

"That would be amazing, Jen. I've only really been in the sitting room for a long time. That could be good fun."

"We could also sit on the green under what we called the 'umbrella' tree. I wonder if it has a proper name."

"Apparently it's a 'Buckeye' tree. It's cut back very heavily now and again, though it grows back incredibly quickly."

"It's a bit like this man then!"

They both laughed as Steve emerged, yawning and wearing only a pair of shorts.

"Sorry, Julie. I forgot you would be in the kitchen, but good morning anyway, ladies," he said before sneaking a kiss from Jen. He was suddenly interrupted by his phone ringing. "It's Chris from the police... Hi, Chris."

"Hello, Steve, and sorry to bother you. We could do with talking to you and Jen today if that's possible, please. Also, have you any idea where Julie is? We're worried as we can't find her."

"First of all, Chris, Julie is sitting next to me at the breakfast table here in Church Lane with Jen..."

"Can I pop over now, please?"

"Well, we all look a bit of a mess..."

"Don't worry about that. I'm on my way."

The three of them looked a bit puzzled. Jen refilled the kettle and checked the cupboard for more tea bags, Steve grabbed a T-shirt, and then the doorbell rang. Jen answered, knowing who it would be.

"Morning, Jen. Sorry to bother you so early, and hello, you must be Julie. Pleased to meet you. I'm Chris."

Steve arrived back in the room.

"Hello. Yes, I'm Julie, but suddenly I'm feeling unnerved. Is there something I should be worried about?"

"There isn't a delicate way to say this, but someone was murdered in your front garden yesterday." Julie stood up dramatically, her chair falling over behind her, and then she was emotional.

"My garden! My bloody garden! How could someone be murdered in my garden? And was it me they were looking for? What on earth is happening?"

Jen moved to hold her.

"Come on, Ju. We're here with you."

Steve discreetly picked the chair up, and Chris knew he had quite a job to do. "We don't know who the murderer is at the moment so it may be coincidental."

"We all know most murders are committed by someone who knows you, so who do I have to be wary of?"

"Are you going to be here for the next few hours, Julie?"

"Stay as long as you want, Ju."

"Thanks. I'll be here."

"Jen, I need to talk to you about your DNA test results, but I need someone from Social Services with me."

"As much as I appreciate those rules, Chris, I'm thirty-two years old now and Janice from Social Services is only a phone call away. She's the person who helped me when I was twelve years old, and when I discovered that my mum had died."

There was a knock at the door; it was Tomi Baker, though she had left Billy in the car, or so she thought: he was having a bit of a nose around and getting the 'lie of the land' and the general feel of the place. Fenningwood was what he would definitely refer to as 'white middle class' and even the prices in the window of the charity shop next door to The Bunch of Carrots seemed rather high compared with what he was used to seeing in Chrichton. Looking up Station Road puzzled him a little.

"Okay, Jen, let me see if I can get Janice on a video call just so that I have covered myself."

She answered Chris straight away and they had a brief discussion before her face appeared on Chris' phone.

"Hi, Jen."

"Hi, Janice. I'm afraid that none of us are dressed yet, but personally I would really like to know the results of my DNA test."

"Okay, Chris will take you through it, although it's pretty brief, and then maybe if I could come over in a couple of hours?"

"That's okay, Janice, and just to let you know, I also have here Steve, who is my husband to be…"

"Oh! Congratulations."

"…Thank you. And my friend Julie from Lost Whistle, who has agreed to be my maid of honour. Sorry, I've missed someone out. Tomi Baker is here from Chrichton Police."

"Quite a party! Over to you, Chris." They all stared at him expectantly.

"To be honest, Jen, it's fairly straightforward. There are three clear links: your mother Laura Greening, who we all know is deceased; a half-brother who is a child of your father, although not much is known about him; then there's your father. His name is George Williams and he is a convicted drug dealer, hence we have his DNA. He seems to have spent a lot of his time in the prison at Great Lingwood with an Eddie Pitcher and a Danny Parker, who we all know or have known for different reasons. We obviously know about Eddie – sorry to bring it up again, Steve – and we know Danny Parker is in custody, though will probably be released today as we don't have enough evidence after yesterday's murder."

"Chris, you're digressing," Tomi said.

"Sorry, everyone."

Janice then took over.

"Thanks, Chris. Jen, how are you feeling?"

"I think we're all quietly stunned if I'm honest, Janice. Come over in a couple of hours like you said. By then we'll be showered, fresh and fed. We may also be full of questions!"

"Hopefully I'll have the answers, Jen. I'll see you in a while."

"Tomi, we have to get going to meet DS Meachant." They rushed to their cars.

"Where on earth has Billy gone?"

And with that, he came running around the corner into Church Lane.

"Sorry, I didn't know how long you would be."

"Don't worry, Billy. Your 'copper's nose' is developing well. Let's find out what's in store for us."

They arrived at Fenningwood Police Station just behind Chris, and in the car park made themselves look just a little bit smarter: tidier hair, brushed jackets, and a quick brush of the shoes. The stuff training school said would be important. They made their way to the meeting room. There were just a few chairs scattered around; the tables were at the side. Billy, Chris, and Tomi entered.

"Good morning, sir."

"Firstly, let's be quite clear: I am not 'sir', I am Pete. You see, I was Billy; I was Tomi; I was Chris; and I was Emily. A job title is just that. You get paid more money, and yes, the responsibility is greater, but I'm just a bloke doing a job. So, on that note, let's get back to the job at hand.

"Rachel Hawley won't be around for a good while, partly because of her mother's illness, though also she has become personally involved by default as her uncle is George Hicks, the journalist.

"Both Fenningwood and Chrichton police services now fall to me for responsibility, though on a day-to-day basis, Emily will be running things. Chris, your time will be shared between the two places to ensure that Tomi and Billy are not isolated, especially given the current major cases. There are still four unsolved murders, and as we're not sure exactly what's happened, let's go and get some results. You're all a great team, you know."

They all felt highly motivated and sat down to plan their next steps under Pete's watchful eyes.

Chris started. "Four people have died: Kath's husband Robert, Kath Megson, Eddie Pitcher, and George Hicks. Is there a common denominator?"

"Maybe we just need to rethink each of the people and wonder what their motivations and fears would be?"

"That's profound, Billy. When we get back to Lost Whistle, who would you start with?"

"Rosemary Crumble, Tomi. I believe she knows more than she's letting on."

"Rosemary? She just seems like an old lady who's a bit of a busybody."

"You asked the question, Tomi!"

"Why didn't you talk about your thoughts before, Billy?"

"DI Hawley always said that when she thought I had something valuable to say, then she would listen. I couldn't be bothered on that basis."

"She's away for a while now so please, share everything."

"When I was having a wander around Fenningwood this morning, I noticed a Caribbean-looking man walking up to the station.

"Fenningwood has very few black people in the community, apart from what I'm told about East Fenningwood, and to be honest the people who live there only really pass through on the bus when they're going to Bunhill."

"Why would they go there, Chris?"

"It goes back to the origins of East Fenningwood as I understand them, Tomi. Social housing was needed across the county it's in, and that area was identified as a potential site. After lots of protests and appeals, the low-level estate was built behind trees, with an all-purpose shop, plus an agreement that people who lived there, and their postcode gives them away, would have to use amenities such as doctors, etc. in Bunhill. Just look at the bus destination: it's 'Fenningwood East' because one local body apparently thought that sounded more upmarket! Billy, you look as if you're bursting to say something."

"Could it be possible that the man I saw was George Williams, and he had come looking for his daughter?"

Pete broke the silence. "You've opened a new can of worms, Billy. I like that, as it gets our minds working overtime, and outside of what we were originally thinking, or what ridiculously expensive consultants would call a 'paradigm shift'. I need to go to a press conference about George Hicks in a moment, though let me leave you with some questions:

"How was Robert Megson actually killed, and by whom?

"The missing quilt comes up often: where is it?

"Was the poisoned letter to Kath designed to make the house empty for some reason?

"Was it really Eddie Pitcher who sent that text message, and if he didn't, who did?

"Why was Eddie killed?

"What's Danny's role in the whole thing: murderer, informer, or decoy?

"Is George Williams a murderer? Did he kill Jen's mum or is he now lonely and looking for reconciliation?

"Are Jen and Julie the innocent pair that they appear to be?

"If George Williams killed George Hicks, why was he at Julie's in the first place?

"Does George Williams know that he has a daughter?

"I must get going now, though. Billy, you appear to have jotted down every word I've said. What's your surname, please?"

"I'm Billy Wallis, sir. Sorry, Pete, sir. Sir, Pete. Sorry, I've got myself in a muddle."

"I think you're one to watch, Billy Wallis. Thanks for coming, everyone."

"Chris, Tomi, Billy: you have your work cut out here. Can I have a report back in forty-eight hours, please?"

"Yes of course, Emily. We're getting on with it now."

*

Janice arrived at Jen's flat, a fairly spartan place, but they were all showered and ready to go. A place Jen really wanted to go was back to Lost Whistle and to visit Quilter's End, and she and Julie were talking about it when Steve ushered Janice in. Jen stood up and hugged her, as did Julie, and the three of them talked about Quilter's End.

"I think it would be a great idea for you to go there and—"

"Well let's go today, Jen. You could stay with me tonight and that would really help me."

Janice smiled and then slowed them down a bit. "Before you get going, let's just talk a bit about how you feel. You've had a lot of news today, and frankly, an extraordinary couple of weeks. What can I do to help?"

"I'm honestly not sure, Janice. Maybe I'm running on adrenaline and at some point it will make me realise. What do you think, Julie?"

"I'm a bit scared, if I'm honest."

"And Steve, you're very quiet and thoughtful."

"I think that sums me up that moment, Jen. I can't quite believe everything that's happened, and I just hope I can help resolve it."

"I can only begin to imagine how you feel, Steve, and what about Jen staying at Julie's tonight?"

"I think it would be good for Jen to see Quilter's End again, and I'm sure Dave will come over so I don't need to be alone."

"Okay, well, you all know that I'm only a phone call away. Do have a good time and please, let me know how you're all getting on."

"Thanks, Janice. I'll keep in touch." They all embraced and she left.

"I'd better get packing, then. Are you sure you don't mind, Steve?"

"Not at all. When you walk up to the station I'll come along and see what Dave's plans are for today."

*

Out of his window, Dave was quizzically watching a Caribbean-looking man hanging around by the station, who then suddenly disappeared. *How odd*, he thought, and then noticed Jen, Julie and Steve walking up Station Road. The girls were just in time for the train, and then Steve popped over to Dave's.

"Something odd is going on, Steve. This man has been hanging about; I don't want to sound racist but he's black and that's very unusual here."

"Thank you, Dave. I must phone the police immediately. I'll explain shortly. Chris, it's Steve Pitcher. I think George Williams may be here at the moment, and he's seen Jen and Julie get on the train. They're on their way to Lost Whistle and Jen's staying at Julie's. They're also planning to go to Quilter's End."

"We're on to it, Steve."

CHAPTER FOURTEEN

❖

Jen and Julie were like two excited teenagers on the train.

"I wonder how different it's all going to look after fourteen years."

"It's funny, you know, Jen, because if things have changed, I suppose I've just watched it as it happened. You'll notice how much people have got older. It's not just me, you see!" Julie laughed and they hugged. When the announcement that they were approaching Scanning Junction came, it was time to change trains.

*

At Fenningwood Police Station, they needed to react.

"Well, you all heard what Steve said: Tomi, can we get a couple of uniformed officers to just be patrolling around Lost Whistle, probably today and tomorrow, and then a couple overnight tonight as well?"

"I don't think we'll be short of volunteers, Chris…"

"Can I sort that out, please? I know the ideal people."

"Thanks, Billy. I see what Pete means."

"That's a relief. Thank you all. I think we should use Pete's list of questions in that order, though if Jen and Julie are going into Quilter's End, I would love to have a look in there."

"That's a really good idea, Chris. Why don't you make an arrangement now so that we know our timescales for today?"

"Sound idea, Emily. I'll do that now."

Billy arranged the uniformed staff for two days and overnight; Chris phoned Steve; Emily and Tomi bonded a bit more. A good working relationship and understanding appeared to be developing, although Emily had to leave.

"We have another two hours here, but I'm wondering whether it's worth going now, as at least then we'll only be about ten minutes away."

"I agree; I'd like to have a nose around there."

"You've become insatiable in this job, Billy!"

"It's just everything that I ever hoped it would be: investigating, questioning, and searching."

They got their bits ready to make the move.

"What time is Danny being released?"

"About now, Chris."

"Is that in Chrichton?"

"It's up by Chrichton North Station now, so about a twenty-minute walk from the town centre."

"I was just thinking it may be awkward if they accidentally meet."

"You're right to be concerned, Chris, but we have no idea what Danny will do, or indeed what Jen and Julie will do."

"Do you think Danny will contact George Williams?"

"I'm not sure he will from the mobile phone that we're aware of, although he's bound to have another one at home."

"And he lives in Lost Whistle!"

"He does, but the difficulty with tracking Danny is that there is no reason to go along Bell Note Lane unless you're a visitor or going to the farm. The village is many centuries old, with buildings dating back as far as the 1400s. We have to be very careful given all of the 'curtain twitchers' as well."

"Okay, let's get to Chrichton and take it from there."

They got on their way.

Jen and Julie were just arriving at that very place, and Jen could see buildings she hadn't seen for such a long time.

"Can we have a look at our old school, please?"

"We can, although it's all gated now so you can't go inside through the front. That said: it still looks beautiful with the 15th-century fascia and all of the modern extensions are cleverly hidden out of sight."

"Hidden out of sight is how I would describe East Fenningwood, Ju, so maybe that's why I felt happy here, or am I just dwelling too much on the past?"

"It depends how you use those thoughts, I suppose. If you dwell on it to the point that you don't really move forward, then that would be non-productive, but if you dwell to decide 'that's how I want the future for myself and others to look,' then that must be a good use of that reflection."

"Those are very wise thoughts, Ju…"

"Quick, Jen. Here's our bus."

They got on board the small, rattly bus with well-worn seats and a very welcoming driver.

"What a tiny bus!"

"It has many tiny lanes to go through, with large overhanging trees, and thank goodness it does. I, and many others, would be lost without it."

"I guess I've become spoiled in Fenningwood because it's so easy to get everywhere, and all of the transport is so modern."

At that point the bus turned in towards its first village community and Jen was suddenly full of memories of going to school. Further villages and hamlets made the enjoyment even better.

Then there was a sweeping left turn.

"Is this Pea Lane, Ju?"

"It is, Jen, and I can't believe you're almost bouncing in your seat with excitement."

"It's… It's… It's just that… Gosh, I don't know how to explain it. I wanted so much for these villages to be the same and…" The bus stopped at the Drunken Duck. "…And this is Lost Whistle." She hugged Julie lovingly, then hugged the bus driver, who felt very confused, though really happy to have unknowingly given someone such an enjoyable journey.

"Shall we pop into the Drunken Duck? I haven't ever been in there before: it was just that building that we could see across the green. I'm also trying not to look at Quilter's End yet."

"Yes, of course we can. At some point I need to get some food from the village shop so we have something to eat."

They spent a short while in the pub and arranged to eat there that evening, then started to make their way to Julie's house, but Jen suddenly stopped.

"This is the green that I remember so well. Our outdoor playground. People in their cars would wave to us, although they were few and far between in this location as the roads didn't really lead anywhere. It certainly wasn't a short cut, or 'rat run' as I hear it called where I live."

"We'll have a look around a bit later, Jen. Let's get rid of our bags and relax."

There was a tiny length of blue and white police cordon tape still attached to Julie's iron gate. Jen ripped it off as it would just be an unnerving reminder for Julie. Her cottage was old, centuries old: thick brick walls, small windows, and the most delightful of fireplaces that she clearly still used. It was cold inside, though, and Jen wished she had brought something warmer to wear. Julie noticed how cold Jen was and promised to light the fire, which was the only heating in the cottage. She just needed to get a few logs in before they took the short walk to Quilter's End.

The uniformed police were discreetly doing their job, as Billy had asked them to.

*

At Chrichton Police Station they were still puzzling over Pete's first question. 'How was Robert Megson killed and by whom?'

"What do you know about the case, Tomi? It's fairly recent."

"I know a bit about it but I was away in Cumbria at the time so it was all dealt with by DI Hawley. She described it as a 'tragic accident' that happened outside Piper's Grip Farm on Low Whistle Lane, which is only about a five-minute walk from Lost Whistle itself. One of the things that I didn't ever understand was the postmortem. The conclusion was that it was a hit-and-run by a vehicle, so it was recorded as 'accidental death,' but when you review the case, it doesn't seem accidental at all. I know that lane is very dark, though with headlights on you would see a person, yet there were no skid marks, which suggests the vehicle didn't try to brake. And then there are his injuries. By 'his', I mean Robert Megson. The only recorded bleeding is from his head, where it hit the ground. Some tissue damage on his upper arm, and a huge amount of broken bones in his lower body are consistent with being hit by a vehicle, but why no cuts from the car hitting him?"

"Presumably he was found dead?"

"Yes, he was."

"You clearly don't think this is correct, so what do we do?"

"I need two answers, Chris: what was Robert doing there at that time of the evening? Why was the impact so soft on the tissue of his lower limbs?"

"Those are great points, Tomi, and can I add one more, please? Who wanted him dead?"

"One main question and such a lot to think about, though we need to get over to Lost Whistle to get a chance to look inside Quilter's End. You ready, Billy?"

"Tomi, I can't wait. There must be something in that big house that has clues for us."

They got on their way in Chris' car, though before arriving at Lost Whistle itself, they turned into Low Whistle Lane and made the short drive to Piper's Grip Farm. The aim was to familiarise themselves with the landscape.

"This could be a goldmine."

"What do you mean, Billy?"

"I can see at least three hidden CCTV cameras. If you remind me of the dates I'll ask for copies and download them onto my phone and the attached hard drive. Leave me here and I'll come and find you."

"Are you sure?"

"Yes, I am, and it should only take me ten minutes, so please don't go into Quilter's End without me."

"We'll go to Julie's first and plan to meet you there."

*

It didn't take long for Julie's house to warm up, and she also had a warm 'puffer' jacket ready for Jen when they went to Quilter's End.

"Why did you stay in Lost Whistle, Ju?"

"I didn't really have anywhere else to go, and Kath felt like a safety blanket. My parents had moved abroad while I was at Quilter's End and didn't make any contact after that. I have no idea where they are."

"That's so sad."

"I suppose it is, though that's my reality and it's been fourteen years now. How long do I break my heart for?"

"Isn't having a broken heart just part of us living our dysfunctional lives?"

"Maybe it is, and quite probably it's me. You have moved on; I never have. Maybe this could be a catalyst for me."

There was an unexpected knock at the door.

"Chris, Tomi, hello. What are you doing here?"

"We still have so much to investigate that we're looking at every possible way to find clues."

"Jen and I will be going to Quilter's End shortly; you're welcome to join us if that helps."

"It would certainly be useful to have a look around, if that's okay. Thank you. Jen, how does it feel to be in Lost Whistle all these years on?"

"I didn't expect to be asked that by a policeman."

"We do care, you know."

"I do know, and you've shown it time and time again; I'll bet it's not a coincidence that you're here!"

"So, back to my question: how does it feel?"

"It's very strange, to be honest. Everything is very familiar in terms of the buildings and the green. I suppose what's really different is that I now view it as an adult. When we were kids we had little space within the house, so the green seemed so huge, but now it seems so tiny. I've been into the Drunken Duck with Julie, so another childhood barrier has been broken down." Jen stood up and started pacing around. "Maybe there weren't barriers at all. Maybe they were my safety net, or maybe it was that I had boundaries for the first time in my life. Up until I was twelve years old my life was chaos, really. I don't blame my mum; my bitterness is towards the people who supplied her and encouraged her: all they wanted was her money. I know that now, but we were just poor and that was my normality. Kath saved me, although I would like to see the whole house. Chris, that's a very long answer to your question, though I hope it helps."

"I'm humbled, Jen, and to be honest, a bit lost for words."

Julie made some tea before they intended to go to Quilter's End.

*

Billy had downloaded all of the CCTV he needed and was now walking to Julie's cottage. The walk took him past Rosemary's house on the corner of Fipple Lane and out of nothing more than curiosity, he turned the handle of her garage. To his astonishment, the door opened and fortunately he was still wearing protective gloves. The sight before him was completely unexpected. A car that was clearly much older than his twenty-four years, and looked as if it hadn't moved for a very long time given the cobwebs and green mould growing on it. The notable thing, though, was on the bonnet: a quilt covered with a selection of bungee ropes. Could this be the missing quilt? But why the ropes? Could Rosemary be involved in a murder? He was starting to learn that anybody could in this new world of CID! He closed the door and then sprinted to Julie's, who was surprised to find an out-of-breath Billy on her doorstep. She ushered him in.

"Tomi." He could hardly speak from running so fast.

"Slow down, Billy. Take a few deep breaths and then tell us… Oh! Why have you still got protective gloves on?"

He calmed himself. Julie got him some water and he spoke.

"In reverse order, then. The reason I still have gloves on is because I forgot to take them off when I left Piper's Grip Farm, and I'm grateful that I did. On the way here, and you can call it nosiness, inquisitiveness or whatever you like, I turned that handle on Rosemary's garage. And the door opened."

"And… And…"

"There was a car in there that could have been as old as you, Tomi…"

"…Steady now, Billy."

"I know. I was only teasing. The car clearly hasn't been used for years, but more importantly, on the bonnet is a quilt and a bunch of bungee ropes. I think we need forensics back here."

"I'll know if that's Kath's missing quilt."

"Okay, Julie, then it's worth you having a look and Jen, please come along, we don't want to leave you here alone. Chris, can you go to the garage? I'll go and see Rosemary so that she knows what is happening."

They all walked along Wind Way with different thoughts: Billy was excited about his new discovery; Chris was trying to work out if any of these incidents fitted together; Tomi was rehearsing her conversation with Rosemary; Jen and Julie were just hoping this whole episode would come to an end.

When they got to the garage, Chris was very clear with everyone: "Nobody touches anything unless it's Billy, who still has gloves on."

"That's Kath's missing quilt. I remember I liked it so much that I took a photo of it."

"Do you still have that photo?"

"Hang on, Chris. Let me scroll through my phone. Here it is!" And she showed him.

"There's no doubting that. Let's leave it all as it is and let forensics produce some facts for us. This is a great find, Billy. Julie, can we pop back to yours while we wait for Tomi, please?"

"Of course. It always feels safer when you're with us."

"Thank you. Once Tomi is back we'll take a look at Quilter's End."

CHAPTER FIFTEEN

❈

Jen's mind was whirring now. What about Eddie? What about Danny? What about George Williams? What kind of people were they? She knew George was her biological father, though hadn't ever met him. She didn't know where he lived, what he sounded like, or indeed what he looked like. He was just a name, and a person that she wasn't sure she would like. Her gut feeling was that he could be ruthless. Danny, she saw as a bit of a lost cause and from what Julie had said he just seemed to lurch from crisis to crisis. And then there was Eddie. Steve's views about his brother had been quite off-hand, although maybe there was a bitterness about the inheritance that was hidden away in Steve's thoughts somewhere. Her impression was that Eddie didn't really want for anything, but then her thoughts wandered. Could he have become embroiled in something that he didn't know how to get out of? She shared these thoughts with Chris before they went to Quilter's End, and his mind was now whirring too, especially with forensics in full flow in Rosemary's garage.

*

And so, to Quilter's End. Julie had been a relatively recent visitor, Jen hadn't been there for fourteen years, Tomi hadn't been further than Kath's lounge, and for Chris and Billy it was completely new territory. What was apparent was that it was a very large house. When Julie opened the door there was a smell of mustiness, the way old buildings smell when they haven't been opened for a week or two, or even more!

"How old is this house, Julie?"

"The estate agents believe that it is 16th century, although I don't know what their basis is for that, so that's the best of my knowledge, Chris."

"Maybe it's the history of the area, or something about the area? Jen, you work at an estate agents. What would be your take on this?"

"To be honest, I just rent out flats and rooms, although there must be a specialist somewhere along the way. To be clear, all anyone wants to know is that they will get their money back if it all falls through, and this is a major investment."

Jen and Julie talked affectionately about their time at Quilter's End, and how caring Kath had been. They supposed their experience was very different to many others who only stayed for a month or two, whereas they were there for six years each.

"So, what about the boys' rooms?"

"I don't think that either of us have a clue, Chris. Do you, Ju?"

"Their world was completely different to ours. I may have glimpsed them playing on the green, though wouldn't ever have known who they were. Kath's husband? He was just 'Sir' on the odd occasion that we saw him. When I reflect like that, Kath had a very strange existence."

"Thank you. Let's all go and have a look."

The boys' bedrooms were stark: a narrow bed, a couple of drawers, and a hanging rail all behind a blackout curtain.

"Gosh, Ju, this looks Victorian compared to our lovely rooms."

Then they found Robert's room, which was grand by comparison: the large, dark wood desk with studded green leather; the four-poster bed; and the grand fireplace surrounds and shelving with decorative edges, some up to head height.

"The decoration on this furniture is remarkable," Tomi commented as Billy went to look more closely, but he tripped on something at the side of the fireplace and put out a hand to ensure that he didn't fall. As he did so, the piece of furniture he had touched moved.

"Woah!" he called out as he found himself on his knees staring at a staircase that had until then been hidden. "What on earth...?" The others all stood there in astonishment, looking – just looking and wondering what to say. Chris broke the silence.

"Could that be a priest hole?"

"A what?" Jen asked.

"I'm no authority on this but I seem to remember from history at school that there was a time when priests were banned because of religious differences, so houses that could afford to, and wanted to, would build them hiding places. I may be utterly wrong, though."

"Let me look it up," Billy said, reaching for his phone, and then confirmed that Chris was correct. "I wonder where it goes."

"Only one way to find out, Billy, and I'll come with you."

Tomi felt glad not to be part of this as she found it a bit spooky. The stairs were steep and a bit like a spiral, though with no handrail. She was told that at the first little hiding place they found there were some old and extremely dusty books, including a very old bible, but at the next there was something completely different. Tomi was now kneeling at the top of the stairs and writing notes as new information was called out.

"The top stone shelf has a number of modern files in it, which I'm going to have a look through, but Billy, what have you found?"

"There are quite a number of bags here, all containing white powder. Some are marked with the letter C, and some with the letter H. Each bag has a weight value on the sticker on it."

"These files have detailed records of transactions received and then taken for purchase by another. The transactions are labelled by delivery number, and with lists and details of where the deliveries are intended for. Tomi, we need some help from drugs experts here. Can you sort that out, please? Billy and I will keep going all the way through the tunnel."

"I'm on to it, Chris, and you two take care in there."

Chris and Billy were surprised that when they got to the bottom it was very slightly wet, and certainly now very dark in there, although a short walk through the tunnel took them to a ladder where they climbed out of a well into what could only be described as an orchard. A complete covering of trees with rotting apples and pears all over the ground. Behind them was a plain green door with

QUILTER'S END

a brown handle. Chris turned the handle reticently and it revealed another stone staircase that took him and Billy up to what seemed like a blank wall. Chris knocked all around. Inside the room Tomi, Jen and Julie were slightly unnerved. Tomi pushed at the wall where a picture was hanging, and a door unexpectedly swivelled, revealing Chris and Billy. They were all a bit shocked by the maze they had discovered.

"I wonder if anyone else knows about this priest hole, Tomi."

"The drugs specialists are on their way and I've had an update from forensics regarding Rosemary's garage. I'm also aware that we need to report back to DCI Emily tomorrow so we need all of this in a way that we can explain."

"I know, and we will do, though we may have to work late tonight. Jen, Julie, I'm sorry to ask this question, but as people who lived here, were you aware of anything related to drugs?"

"No." They answered in unison.

"Thank you, and I hope you understand that I had to ask."

"I can't believe this would have been happening while we were here, can you, Ju?"

"Part of me can't, but the reality is: we didn't know this part of the house at all, and I don't mean this to seem in any way cruel, but your mum was a drug addict and for some obscure reason, maybe this was the source."

"Nothing cruel about that, Ju, and maybe if this is stopped it'll help someone not to die like my mum did."

Tomi needed to talk. "Can I ask you both to leave, please? The drugs and forensics people will be here very shortly."

Jen and Julie walked away. They understood the need for confidentiality, though would spend the walk along Wind Way wondering.

For the police, forensics, and the drugs team, Lost Whistle wasn't the quiet place they had imagined it to be. Chris and Tomi were talking about the evidence from the garage. The fingerprints were predominantly those of Eddie Pitcher, which on the face of it seemed a bit confusing. Then Chris remembered Jen's words: 'Could he [Eddie] have become embroiled in something that he didn't know how to get out of?' Why in the world would he be involved otherwise? Yes, he had lived at Quilter's End for a while, but what really happened with Eddie, Danny and George after their time in prison? And what would bring him back to Lost Whistle that would end up with his fingerprints in Rosemary's garage?

"Maybe Danny is a link that we haven't fully made yet."

"He could be, Chris, but then what was he doing at Eddie's on the day Eddie was murdered? Does Danny have some kind of link with Fenningwood?"

*

Julie and Jen were on their way to the Drunken Duck, on what was now a dark evening, with many things to talk about, when suddenly a car without lights on came at great speed and moved towards them so closely that they had to step onto the green. They both felt more fearful than ever, and the uniformed police ran to look after them. Their meal, although lovely, was overshadowed and after walking back to Julie's under the eyes of the uniformed officers they settled in for what would be a late and restless night.

*

Chris and Tomi were thinking about how they explained all of this to DCI Emily Harris the next morning, when a new lead came in. One of the uniformed officers in Lost Whistle had noted the registration of the car that had moved towards Jen and Julie. Billy updated Tomi and Chris and said he would be questioning the owner of the vehicle, as he believed the owner was probably the driver as well. This added to Chris and Tomi's dilemma: a similar approach to hit-and-run but the two potential suspects couldn't have done it. Eddie was dead, and Rosemary had a car that didn't work. The registration plate gave them a direction. Whether it was the correct direction remained to be seen, but it had to be followed up.

*

Jen loved sitting by the fire at Julie's, and after the events of the day they talked long into the night, occasionally reminiscing, though more of the time they would look forward to what they wanted to achieve. Julie had hardly travelled at all but dreamt of being a travel writer. She had undertaken many writing courses and had been a bigger achiever than expected. She would use some of the money from Quilter's End to travel and hopefully start the new career. Jen was more focused on potentially having a career in Social Services as a way of giving something back, and maybe, although she hadn't properly thought it through, becoming a local councillor.

"They would be very brave steps, Jen."

"So is being a freelance writer, Ju."

"You say that, but I live a very comfortable life. I got married when I was twenty and we bought this cottage. At twenty-three I was widowed after his short illness so there was no longer a mortgage, then to my surprise I got a massive payout from an insurance company that includes a monthly income. I could live here forever and decide to do nothing, but that isn't what I want."

"I'm sorry. I had completely forgotten that you're a widow, I—"

"Don't worry, Jen, and to be honest I was swept away as a young, completely innocent and vulnerable girl by a man more than twice my age. His family, like mine, have no contact with me."

"What about Danny, then?"

"I think he's a person I could do well to avoid quite, frankly. If I'm perfectly honest, I wouldn't be surprised if it was him we avoided on the way to the Drunken Duck."

"But why would he drive at us like that?"

"He may have been trying to frighten us as he knows that we talk to the police, and he probably has something to hide."

"Are we safe here?"

"I'm the only person with keys to this house and the windows would be very difficult to get through given how small they are. That said, now Kath has gone, so has my allegiance to Lost Whistle. I would happily move away."

"Would you like to come to somewhere like Fenningwood?"

"Without wishing to sound rude: it's 'as good a place as any'. I would know people there, it's easy to get around, *but* – I wouldn't like to impose myself upon you and Steve and your friends."

"You wouldn't be an imposition, Ju; we don't have to live in each other's pockets, and if you want to fuel a hobby such as writing, I'm sure there are groups and clubs around. Give it a thought, have a look around and let me ask the sales people what we have on the books."

"I'll do that, though for now let's get one of Kath's quilts, a bottle of wine, put on a film, and snuggle up."

Snuggling up was not how anyone would describe the situation in Bell Note Lane! Billy had checked the car registration plate against the one reported by the uniformed police officer earlier and felt confident and ready. What he wasn't ready for, was the hostility and string of personal abuse aimed at him before he had even had the chance to say who he was, or actually to say anything at all. It took a turn for the worse when Billy was physically pushed towards the steps, so produced his police identity card and issued the appropriate warning about arrest. It was clear to him that this was futile and he called upon the two uniformed officers to help him. After what turned out to be only a matter of hours for Danny, he was back in custody again.

When Tomi was updated by Billy late that night, she knew she needed to update Chris, although she wished she could have told him in person. She longed to be snuggled up, too!

CHAPTER SIXTEEN

❦

At Fenningwood Police Station, DCI Emily Harris was eager to learn about the latest developments and was amazed at how much seemed to have been discovered in the space of just a couple of days.

"We have a dichotomy with Danny: is it safer to leave him in custody, or do we follow our instincts, as we believe he will lead us to George Williams?"

"My view is that you let him go, though for goodness' sake, keep tabs on him. Have you got a tracker?"

"Yes, we have a tracker on his car, and we also have his other mobile phone number so we'll know pretty much where he'll be."

"Do you believe that Eddie killed Robert Megson?"

"Yes, we do, although the forensic evidence show other fingerprints too, and CCTV footage only shows his car. Who else would it be? That leaves the question of why he did it."

"Are Jen and Julie safe, by the way?"

"It feels uneasy there, and Jen needs to get back here."

"Two things, then: let's extend the uniformed people until we are confident that they're safe, and if necessary, one of you two give Jen a lift back here. She needs to know that we're concerned about her. I must also say that this house 'Quilter's End' sounds fascinating; in fact the whole village sounds quite interesting. Maybe I'll take a trip over there one of these days. So, back to Pete's questions. We're confident that Eddie killed Robert Megson, although we don't know why. Robert's injuries were softened using Kath's missing quilt, which although was found in Rosemary's garage, she says she had no knowledge of it being there, and from what you're saying, she probably hadn't been in her garage for a long time.

"I still don't really get this poisoned letter business. It's a very odd happening, and for Eddie to send: 'It should have been him' when he had already killed Robert, doesn't make any sense, although I'm sure when we piece this whole lot together there'll be an understandable explanation. Do you know any more about George Williams?"

"No, is our honest answer. We don't and we need to."

"We all need to, and you've now found evidence that he's part of a drugs chain, so at some point we must confront him, we just need to pick our moment carefully."

"Finding him may be a bit easier said than done, although as we've said, maybe Danny will lead us there. I have a gut feeling he may be around Fenningwood."

"Then go with that gut feeling, Chris. There's more than one crime to be solved here. I shall leave you both to it as you're clearly doing a great job. Can we have another catch-up in a few days, please?"

"Yes, of course, Emily. We'll see you soon."

*

Jen and Julie finally woke up on the settee at six in the morning, as did Steve and Dave in Fenningwood. In all of their minds, so much was going on. People had died and they had unexpectedly become part of something they hadn't ever intended.

In Lost Whistle, Julie got the fire going and brewed some tea, so that by the time they had showered, it would be lovely and warm.

Steve also got the kettle on and Dave was wondering whether he should confess his knowledge of Lost Whistle and some of the goings on, or was it best left as his quiet and very guilty secret?

"I definitely think that you should move, Ju. There's nothing to keep you here now, and to be honest it feels a bit creepy and in the past. I can't imagine a reason to come back here once you have moved."

"I'm thinking the same, Jen. Let's get up and get going. I'll come to Fenningwood today and while you're at work I can take a look around."

"Brilliant. Pack plenty and you can stay at Steve's place, as I haven't got around to advertising it yet. It'll feel much safer if we're all near each other."

"Maybe I should move in there for a while."

"That's a very good idea, then you could decide whether you would like to stay. Once we're showered I'll let Steve know. I have no doubt there'll be tidying up to do!"

*

Tomi was on her way back to Chrichton to update Billy and then find out when Jen needed a lift. Chris was writing on the 'write-on, wipe-off' walls what they knew and trying to make any links. He was starting to wonder whether the CCTV footage that Billy had gained could actually reveal anything else. They were so focused on Eddie's car that maybe they had missed something. He made a note to talk to him about it. He realised that he missed Tomi, as they would bounce thoughts and ideas off each other. Working together clearly had advantages in his view. He was also starting to realise that he enjoyed her company as well.

Steve and Dave were still clearing up from their attempt at making a homemade curry the night before.

"Don't worry, Dave. Jen probably won't be back for hours yet. I'll have a shower and then get some air freshener."

"I thought she said she was working today."

"I think you're right. I need to give her a call." Steve quickly learned that Jen was on her way back and that Julie was going to stay at his flat for a while. "Dave, I need help. They're on their way back. This place needs tidying up and so does my old flat as Julie is going to stay there."

"No problem, Steve. Let's get on with it and make them proud. They've both had a tough time."

"You're right, Dave, and I love the way you talk about them. It's almost as if you've known them for years and I really appreciate that."

Dave's heart and emotions felt heavy when spoke of the two 'girls', though for reasons he hoped never to reveal, not that he ever thought it would stop him being Steve's best man, as they had become so much a part of each other's lives. The truth was, everyone else had revealed their lives, but he hadn't. When would be the right time?

*

Tomi arrived at Julie's in Lost Whistle but it was locked up: no sign of either of them. No clues as to where they had gone. She needed to phone Chris Austen at Fenningwood Police and let him know.

"Thanks, Chris. I was worried for a few moments, then. I also need to spend time with Billy going through what he discovered and giving him some time, then I need to get to Fenningwood to talk things through with you and—"

"Calm down, Tomi. It can all get done. I don't mind how late I work, so if necessary bring an overnight bag. I have a spare room."

"Okay, thank you. I must get back to Chrichton now."

Chris found it unusual that Steve wasn't answering his phone and a worry started to set in. Where was he? What was going on? He'd leave it for half an hour.

The truth was, Steve was frantically tidying his flat for Julie's stay and Dave didn't hear the phone as he was in the shower at Jen and Steve's. He was actually quite surprised at how much he had cleared out, although like Jen he didn't have a lot of 'stuff', it was just things and clothes he needed or wore regularly. He cleaned the bathroom, changed the bedding and after a quick vacuum of the carpets the flat looked perfectly good. It was then, he realised that he had left his phone behind, and had no idea where Jen and Julie were.

Steve ran back to Church Lane and arrived as Dave was drying himself. Looking at his phone, Steve saw that Chris Austen had tried to call him, Jen had also called him, and most worryingly the tracker said that Danny was on the train from Scanning Junction, most likely the train Jen and Julie were on. He first checked with Jen; they were both okay, and again excitedly travelling together. They would be arriving around 08:30am so Jen could be at work at 9 o'clock. He then phoned Chris Austen at Fenningwood Police.

"Sorry I missed you, Chris."

"We wanted to check that Jen and Julie are okay. Tomi has been there but it was all locked up and we're a bit concerned."

"They're both on their way here as Julie is going to stay at my old place in Carrot Crescent for a while, but my tracker on Danny's phone suggests that he is on the same train and it is worrying me. Why is he coming to Fenningwood?"

"Thanks for all of that information, Steve, and I wonder why Danny is coming here too. Could he be meeting George Williams? I'll go up to my flat as that looks over the station and I can check what is going on."

"That's oddly funny. Dave's room overlooks the station."

"I know, Steve. He lives next door."

"Well, who would have known?"

"A 'copper' would. As soon as I've seen them arrive I'll let you know. Just be aware that if no criminal activity takes place, then we won't be doing anything more than watching."

"I do understand that, Chris, and thank you."

Chris updated Tomi, Steve got ready to get some work done, Dave walked home and Chris then made his way back to his flat, seeing Dave as he drove in. He decided to question him in a gentle way: What did he know about Lost Whistle and why? What was his fascination with the 'girls' and how did it start? What was he hoping to achieve? Everything was cut short by the arrival of the train.

"I need to go, Dave, as I want to see what's happening."

Chris ran up the stairs to his flat and saw Jen and Julie come out and walk down Station Road. Then Danny appeared from the station and to Chris' surprise, George Williams walked across the railway bridge to meet him. They talked for a very short time, then walked along the footpath to the common. Where were they going? Chris decided to try and follow them, wondering why they were heading onto the common. He was concerned that Danny would recognise him, so kept a distance, although once they had passed the car park at the end of Common Road, the next place they could exit would be at East Fenningwood. Could they still be dealing drugs there? Maybe they had made a completely wrong assumption that Jen's mum was the only user, and how did Danny know his way through this back route? He surely must have used it before and they were very close to East Fenningwood now, when suddenly they stopped. It looked like, although Chris couldn't be sure, something had changed hands. What it was could be anyone's guess, but then Danny went off and left George in the shelter of the trees. Chris really wanted to confront him but how would he justify it, and more importantly, what would be the impact on the bigger-picture crime? He needed to be careful and just wait.

*

Jen and Julie weren't waiting for anything: Julie had gone to Steve's flat and was sorting a few bits out, as well as thinking about getting some new bedding. Jen was compiling a list of properties with the team, who were keen to help Julie purchase. Steve was off to work after a kiss from Jen earlier, and to be honest, just glad that they were both safely home. He was starting to wonder whether his brother Eddie had any role in the events at Lost Whistle. Maybe he should have stayed closer to him? It was a question that he couldn't answer but was clearly troubling him. If he had been closer to Eddie then possibly he wouldn't have become so involved with the people who ultimately seemed to be the cause of his demise.

*

Cleaning the windows at his first contract, Steve's tears were falling as fast as the water from his sponge. Feelings were suddenly appearing in his world, and it was probably Jen's influence. The warmth and honesty of her was something he hadn't experienced before. She seemed to understand herself, and he wanted to understand himself in the same way. A letter had arrived for him that he opened when he popped back for a couple of minutes in the day, and it was from a firm of solicitors, something to do with Eddie's estate. It would have to wait until later as he needed to get back to work. His next job was cleaning the windows at Snow and Co. so that gave him the opportunity to see Jen at the same time. For so long, he had slowly washed their windows looking at Jen and wondering whether she could ever be part of his life, and now he was preparing to marry her. His life had changed so much in a fairly short space of time. Time now, though, to focus and spend the afternoon working.

*

Chris was entirely focused, his only concern being that he hadn't actually seen George for a while now, although he couldn't have left the woodland area without Chris seeing him. Maybe Danny had more than one client. He didn't even like to think of it like that, so his mind changed the words to 'more than one victim' and he was preying on them. He found that his thoughts were making him angry in a way. Why did people do these things to others? They knew they were killing people and all for the sake of money. If it wasn't for people like this, Steve's future wife could have had her mother at her wedding. Then Danny appeared and produced envelopes; the camera on Chris' phone was working overtime! There was clearly money changing hands and talking that he was too far away to hear. He needed to stay hidden but all of a sudden they split up: Danny walked along Common Road where Eddie had been murdered, and George carried on towards the station.

*

Jen's colleagues knew exactly where they were both going with Julie: she was a cash buyer, wanted to live near the town centre and station, and wanted somewhere with easy upkeep. Steve noticed Julie as he moved from job to job, and his mind whirled away in what felt like emotional explosions inside of him. Maybe he needed to let Jen know just how much he loved her, and how much she had released inside of him. Should he talk to Dave first? But then he thought: what would Dave know? He always had supportive words, though to Steve's knowledge hadn't ever had a relationship, or indeed, suffered any trauma in his life. The truth suddenly dawned that Steve didn't really know Dave at all. They had been friends for a long time but that was pub friends, quiz night friends, that kind of thing. He would talk it through with Jen later.

Steve's next job was at the charity shop on the High Street. He could see Danny inside talking to a young lad. The conversation, although he couldn't hear it, was obviously agitated, and the young boy was acting in quite a threatening way. Steve wondered if his mum was a victim like Jen's mum had been. He phoned Chris to tell him. Whispering, Chris said, "I'm aware of Danny and George but I'm carrying on following George, who seems to be going to the station. I had wondered where Danny would go and now I know: thank you."

To Chris' surprise George jumped on a bus to Bunhill that arrived at the same moment as he did, and then waved out of the window to Chris. George knew that he was being watched; what he didn't know was that he was Jen's father, and by association had killed her mother. Chris then rushed to the charity shop and although Danny had long since left, the young lad was still there looking very scared.

"Hi. I'm Chris, from the police. Are you okay?"

"What do you want with me? I'm from East Fenningwood."

"It doesn't matter where you're from, I just want to help and that man seemed to really upset you."

"What is it to you? It doesn't matter: none of us matter."

"Why do you say that?"

"You let them people get addicted to stuff."

"I don't want anyone addicted to anything. I'm sorry, I don't know your name. I'm Chris, as I said. Is there a problem at your place?" The boy burst into tears and was immediately comforted by the charity shop staff who turned the sign on the door round to read 'closed', despite Steve still cleaning the windows that he had now done many times in a row as he was fascinated by what was going on inside. If only he could hear what they were saying!

Then Chris came out.

"Oh. Hi, Steve..."

"Is everything okay?"

"I need to get hold of Social Services. I think this boy from 'East' has a mum who is a drug addict and—"

"Chris, you don't need Social Services, you need Jen, as that's exactly what she's been through and she's in Snow and Co. now."

Chris ran to find her and she helped immediately. The whole atmosphere in the charity shop changed, as did the boy's demeanour.

"You're one of us, aren't you?"

"I certainly am. I'm Jen from Block Three. What's your name?"

"I'm Sid and I'm from Block Three as well." They fist bumped and smiled.

"Come on, Sid. Let's go somewhere more private, but I need my friend Chris to come with us."

"Is he your boyfriend?"

"No, my boyfriend is Steve who was cleaning the windows. We'll use the room in the estate agents as long as Maddie doesn't mind. Is that okay with you, Sid?"

"I'd like that. You're making me feel safe for once."

CHAPTER SEVENTEEN

❧

Tomi and Billy were revisiting the CCTV from Piper's Grip Farm from when Robert Megson was killed, to see if they could identify the driver, but as much as Billy tried he couldn't get the picture bright enough to pinpoint who the driver was convincingly. This was troubling Tomi as they had told DCI Emily that they were positive it was Eddie Pitcher, but then all of the evidence appeared to be circumstantial.

"Let's go back there and take some photos, Billy. I also want to take a look at the report of the accident to see if the recorded events hang together. I'm having doubts about whether we're correct about this."

"Who else could it be, Tomi?"

"I don't know, but there are fingerprints on that quilt and those bungee ropes that belong to someone we don't know about, but someone presumably knew about the quilt. Who was it?"

"Is it worth talking to Rosemary?"

"I think that's a very good idea, Billy." They got on their way.

"We don't really know a lot about Rosemary, do we?"

"I suppose not, now that you mention it. Let's go to the farm first and then see if her bicycle is there."

*

In Fenningwood, Jen and Chris were finding out more about Sid and his mum, although Sid had struggled to settle down and now sat beside Jen on a meeting room chair, holding her hand. He clearly trusted her, and Chris realised that gaining the same trust from the East Fenningwood community would not be easy at all. The divide was much deeper than he had imagined and his policeman's head thought this could be a barrier to progress, especially if people 'closed ranks', as he was taught at training school. He needed to speak. "So, what went on in the charity shop?"

Sid looked at Jen, almost as if to ask for approval to speak. She smiled at him and nodded.

"After that man left Block Three I followed him back across the rough part of the common and then he disappeared into the bit covered by trees. I know that area well because we play there a lot." Sid's voice suddenly went quieter with emotion. "He met someone, a dark-faced man – much darker than Jen – and something was going on with envelopes. I don't know what that was all about, but then the white man ran to Common Road so I ran after him. I think he clocked me as he slowed down on the High Street, and then he went into the charity shop. I went in too."

"Weren't you scared?"

"I was a bit, I suppose, but I was angry. That horrible man comes round and takes my mum's money for something that leaves her helpless and I wanted to attack him. It wasn't ever going to work, and here I am."

"Can we talk to your mum and—"

"Careful, Chris. Sid's mum probably won't want to talk too soon after a delivery. Let's allow Sid to guide us."

"You really understand, don't you?"

"I hope so, Sid, for the sake of people like you who are going through what I went through. Does this man visit any other places in Block Three?"

"I think there are two others but he only comes once a week. I hate that day: no tea, Mum in a mess, noises from below. If I knew who my dad was I'd ask to stay with him but that won't happen!"

"What would you like us to do to help?"

"Stop the man delivering that stuff, please."

Jen looked at Chris who seemed ready to cry, though spoke all the same.

"We've let you down, Sid, and somehow we will stop this." Once again, in Chris' life the 'bigger picture' had to take preference and he was for a moment struggling with that. He was totally aware that Danny could be easily replaced as a delivery person, as there was always someone else waiting to take the money. Whilst it seemed that Robert Megson had been the source, Chris wasn't convinced that Danny had bought directly from him, in which case there must be a middleman or woman. And where does George Williams fit into all of this?

Again, not a shred of hard evidence. Yes, George Williams met Danny and they walked across the common, but afterwards he got on the bus towards Bunhill. The same could be said for Danny; everything was circumstantial. Was there something staring them in the face that they had completely overlooked by being too preoccupied with former prisoners? He needed to speak to Tomi. While he was thinking all of this, Jen had offered to walk Sid home and given him her phone number. Chris had reluctantly agreed to this but said he would be informing Janice at Social Services.

*

Tomi and Billy turned into Low Whistle Lane and tried to re-enact the scene of Robert Megson's demise, wondering how a car, in the complete darkness, could have avoided driving into the ditch. They took a lot of photos of their re-enactment to compare with the original investigation photos. After this, they stopped in Fipple Lane and Rosemary's bicycle was there. She was delighted to see them and they caught up with what she had been up to, which actually didn't amount to very much at all.

"How are you getting on, Billy? I've only met you a couple of times and that has been quite brief."

"I'm really enjoying it, Mrs Crumble, as—"

"Please, dear, call me Rosemary. That surname haunted my poor husband. His name was Albert but everyone called him 'Rhubarb' and I could see by his face that he hated it, but the people calling him it thought it was funny and didn't see how much it hurt him."

QUILTER'S END

"That's really sad, Rosemary," Tomi said to try and comfort her. "Do you have any other family?"

"Not to speak of and to be honest, I've got used to keeping my own company now."

"Billy was wondering whether he could have a look in your garage. Would that be okay?"

"Yes, of course. There's a side door just here to save you walking all the way round. I'll stay here, or would you like some tea?"

"We're fine, Rosemary, and will probably only be a few minutes, but thank you anyway. Gloves on, Billy." He was gradually getting more used to having to keep gloves in his personal clothing since becoming a detective, as when he was in uniform it was part of the routine at the start of each shift.

In the garage there was the dank feeling of a place largely untouched for a good while, although it had clearly been used to store the quilt and bungee ropes before forensics took them away. They entered through a veil of cobwebs but could easily get around, as the car was parked in the middle of the double garage. Then Billy noticed something.

"Have a look at the key rack, Tomi."

She duly did and they were all covered in cobwebs, bar one: the keys to Rosemary's late husband's car.

"Does that mean that these keys have been touched recently? I suppose forensics wouldn't have needed them as there were already keys in the ignition."

"It could do, Billy. Let's see if the car starts."

The car didn't make a sound, not even a click, which suggested that it hadn't been and wasn't going anywhere. Billy had a look through the glove box, though all it held was a manual, a windscreen scraper and half a packet of unsmoked cigarettes. He tried the boot, but all that was there was a red triangle that looked as if it hadn't ever been used and a supermarket bag for life. Billy and Tomi looked at each other in dismay: they weren't getting any further forward. A promising investigation appeared to have lost its way. They needed to contact Chris.

*

Jen needed to make sure that everyone had remembered the appointment with the registrar tomorrow, and make sure that he or she had all their personal details. It was soon confirmed that they would all meet at the station for the short ride to Bunhill, and it should all be completed in less than an hour. There wasn't a lot else to prepare for the wedding apart from some flowers for their table, as it would only be the four of them, though maybe a conversation with the chef could be worthwhile to make the meal a real treat. For now, though, she needed to get on with some work.

Renting out Steve's flat to Julie had probably saved her performance figures a bit, but she knew she had been given a lot of leeway, and now had to both be, and be seen to be, focused. The last few weeks had been an incredible period in her life; so much happiness to look forward to, although still some ghosts from the past: the drugs issues in East Fenningwood, and what were becoming very mixed memories of Lost Whistle. She had found her love, and couldn't believe how long he had yearned for her. Soon they would be husband and wife. It gave her a glow.

Julie was feeling a glow as well, after seeing and exploring some houses that she rather liked. That said, her feet felt weary, and she had details to read through again. She realised this would be a good move for her. She had loved Lost Whistle but had become almost trapped. Julie was searching for the correct word to describe herself and realised that in a way, she had stagnated into this quiet and unchallenging way of life. It was definitely time for a change: she was only thirty-two years old, for goodness' sake. Time to move on; time to travel; time to write about it. She looked up a stationery shop in Bunhill and added that to her list of things to do tomorrow. So, where should she travel to for her first attempt at writing?

Dave had just finished work, as had Steve, and sent a message to the others. 'I'm popping into The Carrots. Anyone like to join me?' This was all a bit new to Julie as she hadn't been involved in any kind of social life for years. She called Jen to check that it was okay.

QUILTER'S END

"Ju, you are so sweet, and it helps me to understand what a lonely life you have been leading. We do this kind of thing often: spend a bit of time together and then go home for tea. A lot of the time it's spontaneous but I guess we've just got used to it."

"Do I need to get dressed up?"

"You can if you want to, though Dave will probably be in his train company uniform, Steve will be wearing whatever he's been wearing for his cleaning jobs today, and I'll just go as I am. It's you that we would like the company of, not the contents of your wardrobe."

"Thanks, Jen. I'll be there in a few minutes."

*

Chris was delighted to see Tomi's name appear on his phone, and it was quickly apparent that they were both in a quandary.

"What's Billy doing this evening?"

"I'm out tonight, Chris."

"Sorry, I didn't realise that you could hear me. I didn't mean to leave you out."

"No problem."

"Tomi, can you come to Fenningwood and we can go through what we've got on the write-on and wipe-off board to see if we've missed anything? This needs more than one mind and a lively conversation. Also, pack a bag as we may need to find you somewhere to stay overnight."

"I think that could be really helpful as we're a bit puzzled too, aren't we, Billy?"

"Yes, we are. Though I'll have a look through the photos before I leave for the gig and they should be with you before you get to Fenningwood. I'll copy you in as well, Chris."

"Dare I ask who you're going to see, Billy?"

"Probably best not to, Chris, for at the moment you still appear to think that I'm quite sensible."

"Good answer; have a great time."

"I'll be with you in about an hour, Chris, as I need to pop home and get some bits."

"Look forward to seeing you. Safe journey." Tomi looked forward to seeing him so much!

*

It was lively in the Bunch of Carrots and Julie was amazed at how much fun everyone was having: so welcoming; so interested; so friendly. Like nothing else she had ever experienced.

"For once in my life I feel like I'm alive, Jen. This is a whole new world."

"It's only a small world, Ju, though a world where some people are trying to make a difference. Welcome to the next chapter of your life."

"I think this is a chapter I shall thoroughly enjoy, and that will kickstart my life again."

"How did you get on looking at houses?"

"Well, your salespeople certainly prepared themselves very quickly! We started in Common Road where the houses are actually quite large, and to be honest, more than I need. Why do I want to have three bedrooms?"

"A spare room is always a good idea in case somebody needs to stay, and if you're going to be writing, a third bedroom could be your office."

"I can see why you're in this job, Jen. Next we went to Old Mill Lane, which was lovely, although I felt as if I was getting a bit remote from the centre."

"The other thing is, Ju, Old Mill Lane doesn't have any pavements or streetlights so it's lovely in the daytime but at night can be perilous for pedestrians."

"I hadn't thought about that. So then we went off to the far end of Station Road beyond the other row of shops, and that seemed quite nice as well."

"It is, although a long and steep walk home after an evening out: I'd have another look at Common Road if it was me. Would you like me to come with you?"

"I think that would be really helpful."

They were interrupted by Steve.

"Jen, I've just remembered there was a letter from Eddie's solicitors that I meant to look at. I'm just going to pop back and get it."

"Okay, see you in a few minutes."

Dave joined Jen and Julie, who told him about the house she had been looking at. He smiled and was enthusiastic, but inside was envious as he only had a room to call his own in a shared house.

Steve returned with the letter and started reading. Jen could see tears forming in his eyes and put a hand on his leg to give comfort. He put the letter down and took a sip from his drink. Dave spoke first.

"Are you okay, Steve?"

"I think so. Well, yes I am, but then maybe I'm not. I suppose then that the answer is, I don't know."

Julie was struck by Steve's honesty with his friends. This wasn't just a new chapter: this was a new world, and she looked forward to being part of it.

"What has taken you aback so much?"

"It's Eddie's personal words, Dave. They're the words of a sweet and tender man who was clearly very lonely and troubled. There are also words in there that I need to share with police, although that can wait until tomorrow. At the moment only I have read them, although Jen will read them later, then after we've been to the registrar tomorrow I'll let the police know."

*

Tomi arrived at Fenningwood Police Station and Chris was there, pacing up and down by the write-on, wipe-off wall, writing clues at the side. He was visibly frustrated.

"Hello!" Tomi said with a big smile. "Can I join in, please?" Chris was so pleased to see her; he desperately needed another viewpoint. He put his hands on her shoulders.

"I'm so glad to see you. I really need your thoughts, and I know this is not allowed but I could really do with a hug if you don't think I'm overstepping the mark."

"Not at all. We all need affection and a hug is lovely. So, where are we?" They went through the whole investigation.

"For everything that we know, we also doubt all of it. I was thinking about Rosemary's car not starting. Has someone taken the battery out?"

"We need a break from this, Tomi. Let's go back to mine, share a bottle of wine, order a pizza and talk about something different."

They both flopped onto Chris' sofa, ordered their pizza and chatted about their lives. Chris was wondering whether to buy Steve and Jen a wedding present. He got his iPad out to view potential presents and they snuggled closer, clinked their glasses and had the briefest of kisses.

When Chris awoke at 6am, he was still enjoying the warmth of Tomi on his sofa. Maybe there was more than one puzzle that could unfold today!

CHAPTER EIGHTEEN

❖

Jen and Steve were excited. After today, the next time they would see the registrar would be at their wedding, which was very soon now. The four of them gathered at the station for the short trip to Bunhill, which was only three stops away on the train. They were all chattering like schoolkids, although then stopped briefly at the noise of the train pulling into the platform. Julie was thinking about looking around the shops in Bunhill so that she could get a feel for what it would be like to have these things within easy reach. Jen would have loved to show her around but really couldn't take any more time off from Snow and Co.

When they arrived at Bunhill, Julie was agog! She had been used to Chrichton being the big town but this place was massive by comparison.

"We need to walk through the North Shopping Centre and—"

"North Shopping Centre? Jen, how many are there?"

"There's north, south and west; I think there was an intention for an east but the station is in the way. Anyway, we need to walk through north, then it should be the doorway at the side of the bakers."

As they walked through the shopping centre Julie's eyes were everywhere. She would definitely be coming back here.

"Right, here we are then, and to be honest I don't think that this will take long at all."

"In we go, then, wife to be."

Jen kissed Steve and whispered something in his ear; they were both looking forward so much to their special day, and more importantly, their life together.

They were warmly greeted by the registrar who told them that this was a formality and that she was looking forward to the wedding day in Fenningwood.

"I think we'll start with the bride; I just need your full name, please."

"Jennifer Greening, and I'm a spinster. My goodness: I haven't said that word out loud before. I'm thirty-two, but being a spinster makes me sound ancient."

"It's a very old word dating back to Anglo-Saxon times when women were at the spinning wheel, so let's have the bride's maid of honour next, please."

"I'm Julie Anne Miller and I'm a widow."

Steve and Dave looked at each other, shocked by this new piece of knowledge as she, too, was only thirty-two years old.

"Is that Anne with an 'e', Julie?"

"It is, and thank you."

"Now to the groom, please."

"I'm Steven Pitcher, with a 'v', and I'm a bachelor, which sounds far more glamorous than a spinster." He squeezed Jen's hand as a sign of affection.

"And it is. Bachelors were young, unmarried men aspiring to become knights. Maybe you should be on horseback with your bride holding a spinning wheel behind you, and then she symbolically throws it away as a sign of your marriage. Sorry, I'm getting carried away!"

"Don't worry. You sound wonderful for our wedding, although I'm not sure where Steve would get the horse from!"

After much laughter the registrar got back to business.

"Welcome, and how should I refer to you, last man standing?"

"Not at all. I know I'm ten years older than these three, though in our hearts we are all the same."

"That's lovely. So who are you?"

Dave knew that this was a moment of revelation.

"I'm David Albert Crumble."

Jen and Julie looked at each other, almost in disbelief, and then in unison called out, "Crumble?!"

"Yes, Crumble. Rosemary Crumble is my mother. Let's finish here and then I'll explain."

"Thank you, David. I have no idea of the significance of your surname, though look forward to seeing you all very soon indeed."

*

Chris and Tomi were both at Fenningwood Police Station before 7:30am, and again, trying to think through all possible scenarios, but still drawing a blank. How could they have had what felt like so much information, but nothing concrete to move forward with?

Forensics called Tomi about the priest hole at Quilter's End. They had found fingerprints in the folders from more than one person, which they needed to be sure of. Maybe it could lead them to someone, was their thought.

"Do you think anyone else knew about the priest hole, Chris?"

"I'm really not sure, although from what we're told, the Megsons lived almost separate lives. If the fostered boys strayed from their rooms, and I don't believe that they would have dared, they would probably have been punished in some way. What we know is that Quilter's End had a large hidden supply of drugs, and that one person in East Fenningwood has died from a drug overdose, and other drug users there still appear to be supplied by Danny. But Robert Megson died nearly six months ago and we have the drugs he had prepared. Where are they coming from, and where are they stored now?"

"Someone has made the link between the people delivering the drugs and where the new source is. How do we find that person?"

"I'm not sure, Tomi, and without looking back at our usual suspects, what's our plan? Let's go to the café along by the station and have some breakfast, as we ran out of time earlier."

She blushed and nodded her agreement.

On the train back from Bunhill all eyes were on Dave, and all ears were ready for him to explain.

"We're only on this train for another few minutes, so let's go into the station café and talk."

They all agreed and to their surprise, the only other people in there were Chris and Tomi from the police, who were busy in discussion, so they all just acknowledged each other. The four of them ordered their hot drinks and sat down. Julie asked the first questions:

"So, Rosemary is your mum, and you grew up in Lost Whistle?"

Tomi's ears suddenly heard 'Rosemary' and 'Lost Whistle' in the same sentence and wanted to hear more.

Chris hadn't heard anything as the coffee machine was blasting away, so when Tomi said, "Order some more food," he couldn't understand why.

"But we've just eaten."

"Never mind that, we need to stay here so I can listen."

"What are you listening to?"

"I'm listening to a conversation, so let's just look normal."

"I'm beginning to wonder what normal is this morning!"

"Shhh!"

Dave was pondering over Julie's question, and now it was time to tell his story.

"Yes, Julie, Rosemary is my mother and Albert was my dad, and I grew up in their house, The Witch's Wash. Like so many of us I caught the bus to school in Chrichton, although it was a lonely existence. Mum and Kath were dear friends and she was in Kath's house often, though her husband, Mr Megson, was horrible. He always wanted to be called 'Sir', which seemed, I don't know, and I wouldn't have used this word then, but he was pretentious. I may have called it 'poncey' in those days. I knew kids lived in Quilter's End, though I didn't know why. I knew I wasn't allowed to play with them as they were 'special,' whatever she meant by that. I left when I was seventeen, so twenty-five years ago now, and I haven't spoken to my mum from that day to this."

It was Julie's turn to have tears in her eyes. "What on earth made you leave at such a young age?"

"This could be difficult, knowing and understanding what I do now, though this is what happened."

Tomi was completely gripped, and Chris was occasionally hearing what could only be described as the 'edited highlights'! Dave carried on.

"I discovered something that was a village secret, so I banished myself before they banished me. If I were to describe 'them', I think it would be like a group of elders who to me, at the time, had some sort of controlling power over what went on in Lost Whistle. As a result: here I am with wonderful friends and a wedding to look forward to."

They all knew Dave had, in his own way, told them that he wasn't going to say any more, and they respected that. Anyway, it was time to get back to work for Jen and Steve.

Julie asked Dave to walk her home.

Tomi had heard almost everything and rushed Chris back to the police station to explain it to him. Perhaps this new information could be vital, and they needed to get the full story from Dave.

DCI Emily Harris appeared.

"I wanted to let you know that DI Rachel Hawley's mother has died and that she has requested three months off, which we have granted, so the two of you need to be working closely together."

"We certainly are, Emily."

"I can see that by your blush, Tomi, just don't let it get in the way! Can we have a recap in two days' time, please?" Emily hadn't become a detective inspector by chance or without observational skills!

"Yes of course, Emily." She winked at Chris as she said it.

Time to talk to Dave, he thought.

Chris realised that he didn't have Dave's phone number so decided to call Steve. He said he needed to talk about Eddie's letter, although he didn't know whether it had any reference to Dave. He asked if they could both come in, as there may be something they'd misunderstood.

"Tomi's here too, so if we need to talk to you separately then that will work. Can you make 2 o'clock?"

"We can, I'm sure, though you're making it sound a bit daunting. We would all like to get this behind us if we can."

Steve phoned Dave and was a bit surprised to find that he was at Julie's. He arranged to collect him so they could be at the police station for 2:00pm. Julie was fascinated by Dave, as she had lived in Lost Whistle for twenty years now, though he had left twenty-five years ago. She asked him why he had gone away.

"I was uneasy talking about it in a public place like the café, and I will undoubtedly have to tell the police about it this afternoon. Thinking about it, why don't you come with me? Then I only need to explain it once. Also, Steve's going to be here in fifteen minutes."

"Are you sure you wouldn't mind me being there?"

"I know we haven't known each other for long, Julie, but there is something I find really trustworthy about you. I hope that doesn't sound too forward."

"Not at all. It feels very special to be asked."

Chris and Tomi needed to prepare what they wanted to ask Dave about, and were intrigued by what the letter from Eddie to Steve may reveal. Had Dave been involved in some way? Suddenly there were new avenues of enquiry, as they liked to call them. They would have an open room as Detective Superintendent Pete Meachant had advised them to.

Steve, Dave and Julie arrived, and Chris opened proceedings.

"There seem to be two things to cover today: Steve's letter from Eddie, and Dave, your life in Lost Whistle. Some of this could be very personal, so are we happy to expose this to each other?"

Steve and Dave nodded and replied that they were, while Julie looked a bit disconcerted by being there.

"How are you feeling about this, Julie?"

"Honoured, is actually how I feel, Chris."

To Steve's surprise, Tomi was next to speak.

"Can we have a look at Eddie's letter, please?" Steve handed it over and watched their faces. What started as deep concentration turned into astonishment. They both looked up and Tomi spoke first. "Well, Steve, that answers a few questions, though also opens up a few more. Thank you for letting us see it so promptly. Did you know anything about the content of it?"

"No, I didn't. Eddie and I hadn't spoken for years. I did occasionally see him in town, and whilst we would nod to each other, we didn't ever speak; and now he tells of the horrid times he had and leaves all of his estate to me, including what was once my family home."

"Did you know anything about his time at Quilter's End?"

"Not until I read that letter, really, although I had an awareness that it wasn't a happy time for him."

"Dave, did you know Eddie?"

He was a bit taken aback by the sudden shift to being questioned.

"No I didn't, if you're referring to Lost Whistle specifically. I didn't know any of the kids who stayed at Quilter's End; no-one was allowed to. They played on the green but it was girls for about fifteen minutes, then after they had gone in, the boys played for, I assume, the same amount of time. My mum was close friends with Auntie Kath, as I had always known her. I didn't know her husband, although I knew his name was Robert as they always signed their Christmas card from Kath and Robert. However, that leads me to a confession, and what would ultimately be the reason why I left the village."

The room was silent in anticipation of what Dave was about to say next. Julie could only imagine how he was feeling.

"I was fifteen years old and used to go 'scrumping' in the Megsons' back garden, or *The Orchard* as it was known. It had apple trees and pear trees that didn't ever seem to be tended, as there were rotting fruits all over the grass. There was also what looked like a well in their garden with a little ladder inside it. I remember that it was a really sunny day, and when I looked into the well there wasn't any water, and I could see the bottom not far down. I had always thought wells went down a long, long way. I went down the little ladder only to find a short walkway that was still partly lit by the remnants of sunlight coming in through the entrance. Then I got to some steps, where there was light coming from above, and started to climb them. I had no idea where I was except that I thought I had found some secret passage into Quilter's End. Then there was an opening, or something like a hole in the side of the wall and it contained bags and bags of white powder. I had learned at school that bags of white powder were often hard drugs, then I heard Mr Megson's voice and got out of there as quickly as I could. Pinching a few apples and pears was one thing, but drug involvement was not for me: I was terrified." Dave took a sip of water and tears started to fall from his eyes. Julie held his hand. "I kept that secret until I was seventeen; that's when I decided to tell my mum about it but she closed ranks with the village. 'We don't talk about it so neither must you,' I was told. I knew at that moment, it was time for me to leave the village with a dirty secret. That night I packed a rucksack, walked in the dark to Chrichton, which took ages, slept in the station overnight and then got the first train to Chrichton North and asked for a job at the depot, and here I am: a train driver with a room to live in." He was in tears, Julie was in tears and Steve was completely shocked.

"Dave, I... I... I don't know what to say."

"You don't need to say anything, Tomi. I'm sure Chris will have questions."

"Thank you, Dave, and my goodness, that must have been hard to re-live. Where you went in the 'priest hole', for that's what it is, resonated with me as I went down it from the other end only recently. What I find shocking, and there are two things really: firstly, that this drug trafficking has been going on for over twenty-five years, and secondly, that it was known about. Have you ever had the urge to go back to Lost Whistle?"

Dave squeezed Julie's hand for a split moment.

"I hadn't until recently, as the village came back as a talking point.

I went back for a visit with all good intentions but didn't see my mum in the end. I had a look in her garage that I knew would be open, and there was my dad's old car with what looked like one of Auntie Kath's quilts on the bonnet with some bungee ropes. I tidied it up a bit as I assumed it was there to protect the car from frost; then I thought I would try to start it. The keys were covered in cobwebs so I cleaned them up but the car didn't respond at all. Then I decided to leave as I just couldn't face it anymore. I'd asked the cab from Chrichton to wait for me and I just made my way back. I've got the receipt from the cab at home if you need it," Dave said defensively.

"I believe you, Dave, although the receipt would be useful for the records. Why didn't you talk to your mum?"

"With what I know about these drugs now and the end recipients, I couldn't face talking to someone who had kept it a secret for so long, and potentially been complicit in killing the mother of a friend of mine. I may not have much, but I do have principles."

CHAPTER NINETEEN

❖

The staff at the Old Mill restaurant were thinking about Jen and Steve's wedding and what decorations to use on the day. The wedding itself would take place in the Mill Room, so their photos would have the (still working) waterwheel in the background, then they would move to the Mill Stream Room for their private meal, before a small number of guests joined them at the Miller's Thumb, which also enjoyed an outdoor area overlooking North Fenning River. There was a sense of excitement!

If the people at the Old Mill were excited, Jen and Steve were what was often described as 'beside themselves'. Jen was on her way back to work, gave Steve a big hug and said, "I'll be Mrs Pitcher tomorrow!"

"I know, and I'm such a lucky man."

"I'll head off to Julie's about 5pm, then you and Dave are free of us until tomorrow."

"So much has happened, and I'm so pleased that tomorrow is nearly here."

*

Chris and Tomi were determined not to spoil Jen and Steve's wedding but some information was starting to make sense, and people needed to be questioned urgently. If what Eddie's letter had revealed was true, they needed to get to Lost Whistle quickly. When Billy phoned to say that Danny was in custody again after appearing to cause a fight in the Drunken Duck, it was too good an opportunity to miss. Getting to Lost Whistle now had to be fast!

"Billy, can you meet me at Rosemary's?"

"Yes, of course, but I thought you would want to interview Danny."

Tomi gave a précis of the whole situation and Billy got ready to be on his way.

"We'll interview Danny later."

Chris was following Tomi's car in his, though rehearsing in his mind and even speaking out loud sometimes, what he would ask Rosemary. Would it be delicate, or would it be horrible? He felt like he knew a lot more about her after what Dave had said, and he realised that Dave needed to be part of the conversation with her, but he hadn't talked to Tomi about that. He called her, even though her car was only a few seconds ahead of his, as they needed to ensure every piece of information they had gathered was open to scrutiny. Chris and Tomi must not be able to be 'picked off' by a barrister. On this occasion, it reminded Chris that there was an importance to 'the bigger picture.'

*

Julie popped into Snow and Co.

"I think I've chosen my house, Jen. Would you come and have another look at it with me, please?"

"Yes of course, Ju. Which one?"

"Common Road."

"I think that's a good choice, so let's go and have another look."

With Maddie's approval and a Snow and Co. salesperson, they walked along to Common Road.

"This is a great choice, Ju; you could even put a toilet and sink under the stairs to make life even easier."

"That's a good idea. I'll get the deal done here and then get the sale going a bit more on the Lost Whistle cottage, although they tell me that they have already had offers more than the asking price."

"You'll be happy here, Ju."

"I know I will, but now we need to make sure that everything is ready for tomorrow. Do you need to try your wedding dress on again?"

"I probably do. Let's go back to Snow and Co. and get your deal finished, then we can both go back to yours and try our dresses on."

Back at Snow and Co., they were confirming the agreement but reminded Julie that she needed to have sold her property for the deal to be finalised. She asked to phone her estate agent there and then. The salespeople from Snow and Co. listened avidly to the call.

"Julie, we have an abundance of offers, most of which are way above the asking price, so what would you like to do? The moment you say yes, it will be sold, for they all have their finances in place."

"Who do you think will look after it the best?"

The Chrichton estate agent sounded confused.

"I'm not sure what you mean, Julie."

"It's quite a simple question: who will look after it the best?"

"Does that matter when you've sold it?"

"It does to me, but if it doesn't matter to you, then I will find someone else to sell it."

"Okay, I understand. You have three offers at £30K over the asking price, and one at £20K over the asking price."

"Tell me about the buyers, please."

"Gosh, I don't often get asked that. The top three are 'buy to let' clients, and the lower offer is from a young couple, so it's choosing which one of the top three, really."

"Take a moment to tell me about the young couple, please."

"Hang on a tick. Here we go. They are in their late twenties and would like a village location. They can't seem to have children and would like to be part of a village community."

"I would like to sell my cottage to them then, please."

"But that means you are missing out on £10K!"

"No it doesn't, it means that I am missing out on £30K as I would like to sell it to them for the asking price."

"This is mad, Julie…"

"…I am not mad, and if you insult me once again your sale will be lost, and I shall do it privately. Do you want the sale or not?"

"Yes… And sorry, Julie… I was taken by surprise."

"Next surprise then, can you get them on the phone now, please?"

QUILTER'S END

"Now?"

"Yes, now is a straightforward word. I'm in the estate agents in Fenningwood and need them to know that I am a serious buyer."

"Okay, here I go." One of the buyers answered, heard what was happening and agreed to everything. He was extremely grateful.

"Great job. We're done, thank you. What time do you finish, Jen?"

"Five o'clock."

"Dressing up time after that, then!" They both smiled and laughed.

*

Smiles and laughs weren't really the order of the day in Lost Whistle as they prepared themselves to interview Rosemary. Billy, Chris and Tomi arrived at her door. There was something resignedly expectant about Rosemary's mood that in Chris' mind could open up her feelings, but what was the best tactic?

"Rosemary, we need to ask you about a few things, please," Chris started. "Do you understand?"

"Yes, of course."

"Would you like to have anyone else here with you?"

"I could have a lawyer here who would probably tell me to say 'no comment' to every question, but it's probably about time the truth was known, so let's get on with it."

"Thank you. My first question is: do you still have the letter that Eddie wrote to you after the death of Robert Megson?"

"I do. Would you like to see it?" She went to her wooden writing bureau to retrieve it.

"Why did you keep it?"

"Sometimes you feel as if your world has gone mad. Who were these people writing to me? Accusing me of shocking things and I suppose trying to frighten me in some way."

"What do you know about the death of Robert Megson, then?"

"He was killed by a car while he was walking along the road, from all the accounts that I've heard."

"And Eddie suggests that you were in the car with him."

"What would Eddie know? And anyhow, he's gone now."

"How do you know that Eddie's gone?" Tomi seized upon her comment.

"I mean that he's gone from Lost Whistle."

"You're saying that he was here then?"

"I suppose... I suppose he was at some point but..."

Chris toned it down.

"Rosemary, you obviously know about Eddie, and I wonder how much more information we must search for. You have two choices, really: tell us everything and we will look after you as best we can, or stay quiet and we will be forced to take you into custody and apply for a search warrant for this property."

"I'll tell you everything. This could be such a great relief."

*

It was time to try the dresses on in Fenningwood and Julie said that Jen should go first. She took her work skirt and blouse off and Julie was admiring how her white underwear contrasted so beautifully with her delightful brown skin. Although Julie had seen the dress before, after she had zipped it up at the back and Jen turned around, there were tears in her eyes.

"You look utterly breathtaking."

"Thank you," Jen said with a beaming smile.

"The choice of a knee-length column dress covered with lace is just inspired, and I can't think of the words to describe how stunning you look. What do you plan to do with your hair?"

"Same as I do every morning, Ju: straighten it! Remember me as a teenager? I was all frizz and now I wear it long, which I love to do, and Steve loves to run his fingers through it, which gives me goosebumps. Come on then, your turn to dress up now."

They were having such a good time; Julie got undressed and put on her new light blue dress with white daisy shoulder straps. They both went to the mirror and felt very happy with how they looked.

"It's going to be a great day, Jen."

"It is, and I'm so happy. I knew Steve was the one for me a good while ago, but it took time for it to be the right moment for us to get together. Then the moment came and the happiness and love that we both hoped for was there, just waiting for us. Now, let's put these dresses away, get some relaxing music on and check the arrangements for tomorrow one last time."

They sat with a glass of rosé wine each and ticked everything off their checklist.

*

Dave and Steve were far from being in their cosy clothes as they were in the Bunch of Carrots having a pint, albeit running through the key points for tomorrow and making sure there wasn't anything they had missed. Their suits were pristine; shirts carefully ironed; shoes properly polished and cars all ordered. They needed to eat tonight but apart from that, every question was answered.

*

In Lost Whistle, there were still many questions that needed to be answered, though Rosemary had decided to open up about everything.

Tomi started. "How much do you know about the killing of Robert Megson?"

"Everything, dear."

"What exactly do you mean when you say 'everything'?"

"I mean that I know every little detail. I had a plan to kill Robert for two reasons: firstly, he treated Kath so badly, which had upset me over a long period of time, and I mean decades; secondly, the village knew that he was a drug dealer but because people feared him, nobody challenged him. I even lost my relationship with my son because I elected to cover for him. I will never forgive myself for that."

"I assume that you're talking about Dave?"

"Gosh, you know of him. Is he well?"

"Yes. He's the best man at a wedding tomorrow."

Rosemary burst into tears. "I haven't seen him for twenty-five years, you know."

"I know, Rosemary, he told us that. I must ask whether your plan to kill Robert Megson worked."

"Like so many things, you just have an idea in your mind but it doesn't ever come to fruition. I had borrowed a patchwork quilt from Kath with the idea of strapping it to the front of the car and then when I hit him it wouldn't damage the car. But the car wouldn't start, so that was the end of that."

"What did you do then?"

"Nothing, to be honest. For me, the moment had gone."

"Where were you going to do this?"

"Robert's trading was all done in Low Whistle Lane by Piper's Grip Farm; we all knew that."

"What changed and made it actually happen?"

"It was by chance, really. I'd gone out to put some recycling in the wheelie bin and noticed someone near my garage. I called to him to stop intruding and then I thought I recognised him as one of the boys who had been at Quilter's End. 'Are you Eddie?' I called out. 'I am, Mrs Crumble,' he replied, but he looked like a lost soul. I asked him what he was doing here and he told me that he wanted to kill 'Sir' (that's Robert Megson's self-appointed title) as he didn't want to be involved in this drugs world anymore, and he thought the only way to stop it was to deal with the source of the supply. I agreed with him that enough was enough, and there we were, in the dark with a car, patchwork quilt, some bungee ropes and our collective enemy. The time had come."

"Does that mean that you murdered Robert Megson?"

"It doesn't, and there are other people involved."

"Before we get onto other people, are there drugs stored here?"

"No, there aren't, and feel free to search if you wish."

They instinctively knew that would be fruitless.

"So where are the drugs?"

"I'm not entirely sure. Someone else controls all that now."

"And who is this someone else?"

"I don't honestly know. I know Eddie referred to him as the 'connector', although that could be anybody. I don't know, and I'm not sure that I really want to know as he also mentioned Danny, our postman, but where he fits into the whole picture, I haven't a clue."

"Let's just go through Eddie's letter to you. He explicitly states that you killed Robert Megson, and you have openly said that you would have liked to, so what did actually happen?"

At that moment, Billy's phone rang.

"Excuse me, please."

Before Tomi could carry on with her questioning, Billy returned. "Danny has escaped and is causing serious problems at the Drunken Duck. Apologies, Rosemary, but we need to get over there."

It took only thirty seconds or so for the three of them to get there but it was chaos. Two uniformed officers were there, but this had turned into a brawl. Why would such a thing happen in a village pub? Between the five police they managed to get the situation under control but then needed to sort the whole mess out. Danny was handcuffed and in the back of the marked police car ready for the two uniformed officers to take him back to Chrichton for yet further charges! Billy, Chris, and Tomi spent most of the next two hours taking statements from a whole variety of people and then decided to get back to where they had left Rosemary, but she and her bicycle were gone!

"So, what do we do now, Tomi?"

"Someone needs to wait for Rosemary to emerge, as she probably isn't far away. Billy, as you asked, can you sit on a bench on the green? You'll undoubtedly see her, and you can carry on where we left off. I'll leave you my car and get Chris to drop me off in Chrichton. Chris, you need to re-examine our wall chart to see if we've missed something. I know we're going over it time and again but bit by bit, the evidence is being teased out. In the meantime, I'll be interviewing Danny about how he got out, and then why he appears to have caused a disturbance at the Drunken Duck. Let's have a video call at 08:00 in the morning, which will include a review of our inevitable phone calls this evening." Tomi's leadership skills were starting to blossom.

*

In Fenningwood, life was a lot calmer: Jen and Julie had cooked a pasta meal and were on the settee with a second glass of rosé each, both now in their pyjamas and ready to watch a fun film. Dave and Steve had settled on a bottle of red wine with a pizza and were chatting to each other in more depth than they ever had before. By the time Steve got married tomorrow, maybe Dave would actually be the best man he had ever met.

*

In Lost Whistle, Billy was bored! The Drunken Duck was back to being quiet, and there was still no sign of Rosemary. Then, to Billy's surprise, a light came on in Quilter's End. He couldn't see anyone walking around but what did this mean? Either someone had got in through the priest hole, someone other than Julie (who he knew was in Fenningwood) had a key, or someone had broken in. He doubted the latter given the police presence around the village today, and although it wasn't known how many people were aware of the priest hole, it seemed an extremely unlikely scenario. So, the most likely explanation was that Rosemary had a key and was in there. His dilemma was: did he knock on the door and confront her, or wait until the morning when she may have calmed down? Time to consult Tomi and get her opinion, but her phone wasn't answered. He phoned the duty sergeant to ask if she had been seen.

"She's interviewing Danny Parker currently, so how long she will be is anyone's guess, Billy. Anything I can help with?

"No, you're okay. Thanks." Billy phoned Chris and they were of the same view: let her calm down and see her in the morning. "I'll wait and watch her go to be certain that it's definitely her, though."

"You're a good man, Billy."

Rosemary peeped out, wondering when it would feel safe to go home.

CHAPTER TWENTY

❖

Jen peeped out. Today was her wedding day. She remembered those times at Quilter's End when she used to look over the green. There were dog walkers and a lady on a bicycle. In the next room to her was Julie Miller. Despite having married, Julie hadn't ever changed her surname. She also remembered looking out at the playground in East Fenningwood.

Jen then had a sudden compulsion. She showered, dried, straightened her hair and chucked some casual clothes on.

"What on earth is going on, Jen?"

"I want a couple of people from East Fenningwood to be at my wedding party so I'm going to ask them. I'll see you in less than an hour." Julie was in admiration: on her wedding day, Jen still wanted to give and involve people.

Jen walked up Carrot Crescent to South Road and then strode along East Lane towards East Fenningwood with her head held high, and entered Block Three, where she had once lived. Sid answered the door, though his mum Bethany was concerned about who he was speaking to and was protective and wary, until Jen spoke. "I know you probably don't trust me but I mean you no ill."

"Hello, Jen!" Sid shouted, as good as confirming to his mum that Jen should not be feared.

"How can we help you, Jen?"

"I'm getting married at midday and after that, four of us will be having a private meal, and then there will be a few special people joining us at about 1:30pm. You're from Block Three like I was, so that makes you special. Will you join us, please?" Sid was bouncing with excitement!

"Yes please, Mum, yes please."

Bethany had tears running down her face. "I have nothing to wear, Jen."

Yes you do, just come as you are. Promise me that you'll be at the Old Mill at 1:30pm?"

"I promise, Jen."

"That's a good job, then. Now I need to go home and get ready."

"I can't believe that you've come round on your wedding day."

"Now it's your turn to come along on my wedding day, then! See you in a while."

Julie felt a bit frantic by the time Jen got back. "Where on earth have you been?"

"I told you I was going to East Fenningwood and I've invited Sid and his mum to join us after the meal today."

"What a lovely thing to do," she said, calming down completely and once again feeling admiration for her dear friend.

"Thank you, though I think we need to start getting ready: I'm getting married in less than two hours!"

Steve and Dave were thinking the same thing, but then Steve surprised Dave.

"Before we get our suits on I'd like to walk up Common Road and have a look at Eddie's house."

"It's actually your house now, Steve, though let's take a stroll along there; I hear Julie has bought the house next door."

"I'm sure you'll get to know it well, Dave!"

"With a little luck, yes I will."

"Are you a quiet rascal?"

"Not at all. I'm a bit of a lonely soul who kept a secret for too long, to be honest. It's only since I've met you and Jen, and now Julie, that I'm opening up, and most importantly, feel allowed to open up."

"I'm glad that you have."

QUILTER'S END

Steve paid his respects to Eddie in his own way and they both wandered back to Church Lane to get ready for the wedding.

Billy, Chris and Tomi were at Rosemary Crumble's.
"After we got called away, you disappeared. Where did you go?"
"I had some business to deal with."
"Really? What kind of business?"
"I needed to make sure that Quilter's End was safe."
"Who would it need to be safe from?" Tomi was on a roll!
"There was a person that Robert Megson worked with, or was associated with, who wanted to gain access to Quilter's End after he had died. Danny seemed to have dealings with the person and they briefly used my shed, although what went on in there I wouldn't know, and I really don't want to know."
"So, who is the mystery person?"
"I wish I could tell you but I have no idea. My gut feeling is that he or she is a somewhat ruthless person, and probably someone that I wouldn't want to meet, although I suppose that's just me being me."
"I'm going to level with you, Rosemary: I think that you killed Robert Megson. I doubt that I could ever prove it, and I doubt that you would ever admit to it. Kath Megson, Eddie Pitcher and George Hicks are very different cases, though, so we need to get back to Fenningwood to take the whole picture further."

They actually needed to get on their way as Billy, Chris and Tomi had another appointment!

*

Jen's next appointment was with her in-house hairdresser. Julie was straightening Jen's hair for the second time today, and just in time. The taxis were arriving in Carrot Crescent and Church Lane ready to take them for the big moment at the Old Mill. Jen was delighted and surprised that her taxi had white ribbons on it, and made a mental note to thank them after the wedding. They both got their dresses on and were ready to go. Inside the back of the cab was a posy of white flowers adorned by some green leaves, all in a container holding two glasses of freshly poured champagne.

"Congratulations, Jen."

"Thanks, Alex; you've made this very special."

"It really is my pleasure."

Jen and Julie sipped champagne and held hands while Alex gently drove them to the Old Mill where some of the staff had gathered as a welcome party and the doorway was festooned with a variety of bright decorations. Jen was starting to feel a bit overwhelmed.

*

Steve and Dave were already in the Mill Room where the Old Mill, dating back to the mid-eighteenth century, had been reliant upon the North Fenning River, and that in turn had been the key to its success at the time. Its success now was based upon events, and today was one of them.

The registrar and her administrator were fully prepared, and from their experience sensed Jen's arrival was imminent. Steve had arranged for the song, 'You Make Me Feel Brand New' to be playing quietly through the speakers as Jen walked in. A tear was aching to fall from one of her eyes but she wished for it to wait for a while. The ceremony was short, formal, and conclusive. Jen was now Mrs. Pitcher and everyone was delighted. They moved into the Mill Stream Room for their private meal. The occasion had been everything they had hoped for, though Jen was still a bit anxious about the brief after-party.

*

Billy, Chris and Tomi were very anxious too. The background investigations had revealed so much and got them involved with a neighbouring force. Emily and Pete from Fenningwood, along with another force, had decided what was going to take place, and all three of them would be part of it. This was the moment!

There were probably twenty officers involved, some at the rear and side of the property to cut off any escape routes, but most were at the front to ensure the arrest took place. None of the three of them had experienced anything like this before. Then there was a shout out.

"GO! GO! GO!"

With that, police started banging on doors. Amidst the furore, someone appeared and was arrested.

"You do not have to say anything..." And she finished. Approval was nodded and the arrested person was put into a van with a cage in the back. The suspect, after all, had been charged with three murders. At Bunhill Police Station the duty sergeant made the charges clear and then arranged for certain items to be removed and recorded before the suspect was moved to a cell.

"Over to you. It's your case," said the inspector from Bunhill.

"Thank you."

"We're here if you need us, Tomi."

*

Everyone had now arrived at the Old Mill after they had finished their lunch, and Jen's quiet anxiety was quelling. Steve hugged her, Julie hugged her, Sid hugged her, as did his mum Bethany. Sid also hugged Steve, remembering that he had helped him.

In the background a piano was gently being played, with sensitive sounds from the cellist by his side. Jen put her arms up to Steve's neck to hold him affectionately and nodded at the pianist. The cellist stood and took the microphone. The ballad was unmistakable and she sang the words that Jen wanted to say to Steve: 'At Last' – an Etta James song that she had loved for so many years. It was Steve's turn to look at her in an admiring way once again. What a lucky man to have such a thoughtful wife. *Wife. Wife?* Gosh, he didn't ever imagine that someone would ever want to marry him. Jen's truth was in its own way magical, and their dance was as special as they could ever have hoped it would be.

*

In the interview room at Bunhill Police Station, truth didn't seem to be in abundance, though their suspect had some magical theories, none of which seemed to bear any relation to the evidence presented. The duty solicitor asked for some time with his client and he was granted thirty minutes. Enough time for Billy, Chris and Tomi to ensure they were following the correct procedures. They sought input from the inspector, who reassured them. Chris contacted DCI Emily Davies with an update and she accepted the offer of getting over there. He needed someone that he knew well. Tomi agreed.

It was time to re-enter the interview room, and you could have heard a pin drop! As they walked in, the two faces at the other side of the table stared, but there wasn't any engagement, and no sense of emotion.

*

At the Old Mill, emotions were at their warmest and most exciting. The two musicians were playing some wonderful music, then every now and again the cellist would leave her seat and sing to everyone. It was a small, though special group of people celebrating together, and Jen was holding Steve tightly.

"Tonight we begin our lives as Mr and Mrs Pitcher, and I am the happiest person in the world."

Steve's tears expressed his emotions. It was a scene of happiness and joy that many of the staff hadn't witnessed before, and would carry on longer than anyone had anticipated.

*

There were no scenes of happiness and joy at Bunhill Police Station, and Chris and Tomi were feeling more and more frustrated by the words 'no comment' arriving in their ears again. Billy, as an onlooker, was learning so much. They decided to have a twenty-minute break and during that time, talked to, and intently listened to DCI Emily Harris. It was inspirational. When they returned to the interview room, Chris was ready for his big moment with their key suspect.

"I believe you have been dealing in drugs for a long time. You had, from your point of view, the misfortune to have been caught in possession of class-A drugs and ended up in Great Lingwood Prison. You needed 'runners' to deliver drugs and made friends with, or I would say, recruited Eddie Pitcher and Danny Parker, who were short-term prisoners and needed cash at the time, so agreed to be part of your supply chain. However, Eddie's inheritance finally arrived and the debts he had accumulated could be paid off so he no longer needed you, but you wouldn't let him go and threatened him. His answer? Get rid of Robert Megson, your supplier, and the chain would be broken. I'm not completely sure who killed Robert Megson, though I don't think that it was you, but you did need access to the drugs and records regarding them and you were convinced they were somewhere in Quilter's End. If it pleases you: you were entirely correct because we have them all, and you have no idea how easily accessible they could have been. But you needed to find a different way in, so you persuaded Danny to get involved with Julie Miller in the belief that she would have a key to Quilter's End, and perhaps some inside knowledge. Your mistake was that only boys being fostered there would have any hint of what was going on. Then you got Danny to deliver the poisoned letter, as that would mean Quilter's End would be clear of people and you could have a look around. But how? You weren't aware of the priest hole and as well as Julie, Rosemary also had a key, but you never thought to ask her, even though you threatened her enough that you used her shed as a storage site and had free access. She had known about the drugs and the priest hole for a very long time, as her now-estranged son had told her about it some twenty-five years ago. When you arrived at Julie's she wasn't at home, then George Hicks arrived at the same time, recognised you and ended up being killed by you, using the same remarkably similar and sinister method that you had employed to kill Eddie Pitcher. How would I describe these killings then? I think Kath's killing is a simple case of murder. You intended to do it and got Danny to carry out the final act for you. We will question him further about that. The murder of Eddie Pitcher was premeditated, in my view, as he was objecting to what you were doing and as a result, became a target. George Hicks: I think he was just in the wrong place at the wrong time, but you killed him, and that is how you have behaved. The drugs you have supplied have, and continue to wreck the lives of people and their families. I am firmly of the belief that the drugs you supplied in East Fenningwood killed the mother of your daughter. How do you plead?"

George Williams looked up with sadness in his eyes and spoke some words other than 'no comment.' "I didn't know that I had a daughter. Is she okay?"

Tomi took over as Chris needed a few moments to himself.

"She is doing well and she has got married today, so is probably having an amazing time. Anyway, that's as may be, George. How do you plead?

"I'm no good: no good!"

"I'll take that as guilty and remind you of the charges: The murders of Kath Megson, Eddie Fletcher, and George Hicks. You will now be taken back to the cells."

George was shocked to find out that he had a daughter. Maybe she could rescue him.

*

Steve's phone rang; it was Chris Austen from the police. He put his phone onto loudspeaker.

"Firstly, congratulations to you and Jen and my apologies for interrupting you on your wedding day, but we have pretty much concluded the case with George Williams, Jen's father, who is the main culprit. Would Jen like to hear anything further?"

"No thanks, Chris. I loved my mum, Laura Greening, and to me, he ruined her. Justice needs to be done."

ABOUT THE AUTHOR

Garry began by writing songs and poems, then short stories started to be formed, and now a novel. He grew up in North London and now lives in Buckinghamshire.

Printed in Great Britain
by Amazon

d3eba72f-4f4e-454f-aa8a-5793ad7fb97dR01